Time hadn't dimmed the forbidden attraction.

The attraction Dillon had felt for Ashley Wilde back in the days when he'd been Riverton High's resident juvenile delinquent and she'd been its perennial homecoming queen.

If anything, his lust felt more urgent than ever. And the prospect of being locked away in the wilderness with Ashley made his jaded heart skip several beats.

Ashley was clearly as sassy and arrogant as ever. She had the demeanor of a queen, a woman used to being admired.

That alone was enough to make Dillon want to claim her. He wanted her all mussed up and submissive in his bed, the way she was always meant to be.

Dillon suddenly felt like the town's bad boy all over again.

And he loved

Because this t nake
Ashley Wilde

D1416522

Watch as three sisters fall in love with the men of their dreams and walk down THE BRIDAL PATH.

Dear Reader,

March is a month of surprises and a time when we wait breathlessly for the first hints of spring. A young man's fancy is beginning to turn to love…but then, in each Special Edition novel, thoughts of love are everywhere! And March has a whole bouquet of love stories for you!

I'm so pleased to announce that *Waiting for Nick* by Nora Roberts is coming your way this month. This heartwarming story features Freddie finally getting her man…the man she's been waiting for all of her life. Revisit the Stanislaskis in this wonderful addition to Nora Roberts's bestselling series, THOSE WILD UKRAINIANS.

If handsome rogues quicken your pulse, then don't miss *Ashley's Rebel* by Sherryl Woods. This irresistible new tale is the second installment of her new series, THE BRIDAL PATH. And Diana Whitney concludes her PARENTHOOD series this month—with *A Hero's Child,* an emotionally stirring story of lovers reunited in a most surprising way.

Three veteran authors return this month with wonderful new romances. Celeste Hamilton's *Marry Me in Amarillo* will warm your heart, and Carole Halston dazzles her readers once again with *The Wrong Man…The Right Time.* Kaitlyn Gorton's newest, *Separated Sisters,* showcases this talented writer's gift of portraying deep emotion with the joy of lasting love.

I hope that you enjoy this book, and each and every story to come!

Sincerely,

Tara Gavin,

Senior Editor

Please address questions and book requests to:
Silhouette Reader Service
U.S.: 3010 Walden Ave., P.O. Box 1325, Buffalo, NY 14269
Canadian: P.O. Box 609, Fort Erie, Ont. L2A 5X3

SHERRYL WOODS

ASHLEY'S REBEL

Published by Silhouette Books
America's Publisher of Contemporary Romance

If you purchased this book without a cover you should be aware that this book is stolen property. It was reported as "unsold and destroyed" to the publisher, and neither the author nor the publisher has received any payment for this "stripped book."

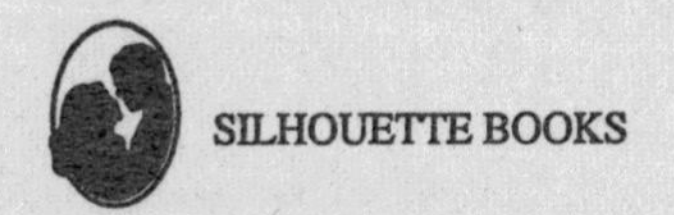

ISBN 0-373-24087-2

ASHLEY'S REBEL

Copyright © 1997 by Sherryl Woods

All rights reserved. Except for use in any review, the reproduction or utilization of this work in whole or in part in any form by any electronic, mechanical or other means, now known or hereafter invented, including xerography, photocopying and recording, or in any information storage or retrieval system, is forbidden without the written permission of the editorial office, Silhouette Books, 300 East 42nd Street, New York, NY 10017 U.S.A.

All characters in this book have no existence outside the imagination of the author and have no relation whatsoever to anyone bearing the same name or names. They are not even distantly inspired by any individual known or unknown to the author, and all incidents are pure invention.

This edition published by arrangement with Harlequin Books S.A.

® and TM are trademarks of Harlequin Books S.A., used under license. Trademarks indicated with ® are registered in the United States Patent and Trademark Office, the Canadian Trade Marks Office and in other countries.

Printed in U.S.A.

Books by Sherryl Woods

Silhouette Special Edition

Safe Harbor #425
Never Let Go #446
Edge of Forever #484
In Too Deep #522
Miss Liz's Passion #573
Tea and Destiny #595
My Dearest Cal #669
Joshua and the Cowgirl #713
**Love* #769
**Honor* #775
**Cherish* #781
**Kate's Vow* #823
**A Daring Vow* #855
**A Vow To Love* #885
The Parson's Waiting #907
One Step Away #927
Riley's Sleeping Beauty #961
†*Finally a Bride* #987
‡*A Christmas Blessing* #1001
‡*Natural Born Daddy* #1007
‡*The Cowboy and His Baby* #1009
‡*The Rancher and His Unexpected Daughter* #1016
***A Ranch for Sara* #1083
***Ashley's Rebel* #1087

Silhouette Desire

Not at Eight, Darling #309
Yesterday's Love #329
Come Fly with Me #345
A Gift of Love #375
Can't Say No #431
Heartland #472
One Touch of Moondust #521
Next Time...Forever #601
Fever Pitch #620
Dream Mender #708

Silhouette Books

Silhouette Summer Sizzlers 1990
"A Bridge to Dreams"

*Vows
†Always a Bridesmaid!
‡And Baby Makes Three
**The Bridal Path

SHERRYL WOODS

lives by the ocean, which, she says, provides daily inspiration for the romance in her soul. She further explains that her years as a television critic taught her about steamy plots and humor; her years as a travel editor took her to exotic locations; and her years as a crummy weekend tennis player taught her to stick with what she enjoyed most: writing. "What better way is there," Sherryl asks, "to combine all that experience than by creating romantic stories?" Sherryl loves to hear from her readers. You may write to her at P.O. Box 490326, Key Biscayne, FL 33149. A self-addressed, stamped envelope is appreciated for a reply.

Trent Wilde
cordially
invites you
to roar down
the bridal
path with
Ms. Ashley Wilde
and
Mr. Dillon Ford

Chapter One

Her face had been on the cover of every important fashion magazine in the world. Her long, lithe body had been photographed in everything from slinky lingerie to even slinkier designer gowns. Her perfectly manicured hands had flashed diamonds and displayed crystal bottles of outrageously expensive French perfume in very classy television commercials. Shampoo and hair-coloring companies had pleaded with her to tout their products as the sole reason for the shining beauty of her waist-length, silky blond hair.

Today, however, Ashley Wilde looked and felt like hell. And today was marginally worse than yesterday, she thought miserably as she huddled in an oversize chair in front of the fireplace in her father's fishing cabin. By the end of the week she could probably become a poster woman for mid-life crisis sufferers everywhere. And she was only twenty-six. What would she look like by the time she actually hit mid-life?

It had been two weeks since she'd fled New York, two months since her traitorous, high-power agent had suggested that her modeling career was all but over unless she could permanently shed ten—okay, fifteen—extra pounds that the camera doubled into thirty. For a man who'd fought like a demon to sign her, he was awfully quick to suggest she was on the skids.

To give him the benefit of the doubt, maybe he'd only hoped to snap her back to reality with his dire warning. Instead, he had plunged her into despair.

Six weeks later, after only a handful of photo shoots, compared to the dozens she usually had, she had begun to take him seriously. When he'd offered her an assignment for a plus-sizes catalogue, she'd blistered his ears with her opinion of his representation, then hung up on him. Blaming the messenger had seemed the logical thing to do at the time.

As absurd as it seemed in retrospect, that night she had stared at her hundred-and-thirty-three-pound image in the mirror and seen a blimp rather than a beautiful, five-foot-nine-inch woman in the prime of her life.

Suddenly the rigid dieting, the even more rigorous exercise and the obsession with appearance had all seemed to be too much. Convinced she couldn't face one more lettuce leaf or one more step-aerobics class or one more snippy photographer's comment about the extra pinch of weight on her narrow hips, she had flown home to Wyoming to take stock of her priorities. Despite all the magazine covers, all the worldwide acclaim, she felt like a failure.

That had been a first for a woman who had grown up believing she was close to perfect, incapable of messing up. For a few moments she had actually resented her parents, her sisters, her teachers and every single tongue-tied boy at Riverton High who'd contributed to the building of her self-esteem. The fall from grace had felt far worse because she'd been so sure it could never happen in her charmed existence.

Yet Riverton was where she chose to go to nurse her wounds. She had spent the first night at home at Three-Stars Ranch, in her old bed, in her old room. She'd expected to feel safe, secure, maybe even beautiful again.

Instead, surrounded by framed covers of other models she'd once collected to inspire herself, she'd sunk even more deeply into her depression. By morning she had been knee-deep in feelings of inadequacy. She had refused every single one of the invitations that had started pouring in the minute people learned of her return.

Besides that terrible sense that she'd lost the woman she had once been, knowing that the ranch now belonged to her sister Sara and Sara's husband, Jake, also made a difference. She had felt as if she was underfoot in the middle of their honeymoon, though both of them kindly denied it. The solace she had sought at Three-Stars simply wasn't there.

As if all that weren't bad enough, her oldest sister, Dani, insisted on hovering. Dani had always been able to see straight through her. No matter how adept Ashley was at hiding her emotions from others, Dani could always detect the truth. She had guessed at once that Ashley's too-bright smiles and too-loud laughter were meant to conceal some deeper hurt. Her gentle, well-meaning prodding had begun over Ashley's welcome-home dinner and showed no signs of letting up anytime soon.

After insisting there was nothing to talk about for the hundredth time, Ashley had packed her bags once again and taken off for her father's secluded fishing cabin. She'd left in the middle of the night to avoid another round of questions she couldn't—or didn't want to—answer. Her thank-you note, left on the kitchen table, hadn't mentioned her destination or her reason for fleeing.

How could she tell Dani and Sara that she, the perfect one, the family success story, had been essentially dismissed from her glamorous career? How could she explain that she'd suddenly developed an insatiable craving for real food and had gained a few pounds as a result of it? No one who wasn't in the business could possibly understand how a few extra ounces here and there could be the difference between stunning success and abysmal failure.

Besides, she was certain that a few days alone in the wilderness would straighten her right out. She would recall the long list of reasons she'd had for going into modeling in the first place. She would remember her desperate desire to flee Wyoming and become somebody. With her resolve intact, she'd have those pounds off in no time and be back in front of a camera quicker than anyone could say, "Smile, please."

That was the plan, anyway. Unfortunately, the solitude wasn't exactly working the magic she'd hoped for. She had a cold that could fell a linebacker. Her million-dollar legs had a rash that she probably owed to a patch of poison ivy she'd missed until it was too late. She hadn't caught a fish since the first day. She'd thrown him back, but he'd probably told all the other fish in the stream to stay the heck away from her.

And, just to add to the general air of gloom, it had been raining cats and dogs for the past twenty-four hours.

As if that weren't bad enough, she was jumping at every snap of a twig, at every whisper of wind. For a woman who'd blithely braved the New York subway and the equally treacherous Paris fashion runways, she was behaving like a ninny. After living in a world of constant noise, she found the silence of the woods nerve-racking.

The lack of television or radio was more disconcerting than she'd expected. Her father's collection of books, which tended toward ranching and fishing treatises, provided no distraction at all.

She'd cleaned the small cabin from top to bottom and unless she did it all over again, she was fresh out of things to occupy her time. The only thing left was thinking, and she wasn't crazy about the direction of her thoughts these days.

All in all, rather than a renewed sense of peace in this serene setting, she was finding her own company unsettling. For the first time in her carefully plotted life, she simply no longer knew who she was.

A soft thump interrupted her thoughts and made every muscle in her body tense. A second thump, even more distinct than the first, had her searching for the baseball bat that hadn't been far from sight since the moment she arrived. It was the weapon of choice for a woman who abhorred guns and couldn't imagine jabbing another human being with a knife.

She inched toward the window and peered into the gathering darkness outside. Eerie shapes and shadows wavered with the slightest hint of breeze. Sheets of rain pounded down with such fierce intensity that she shivered, even though the blazing fire had warmed the room to a comfortable temperature.

A muttered curse in a distinctly masculine tone made her grab the reassuringly solid bat. In her determined hands, it was weapon enough for anyone brash enough to try to enter the rapidly darkening cabin.

Another curse, followed by another series of thumps against the wooden deck, had her heart pounding unsteadily. She decided the bat might not be enough. Perhaps an offensive attack would scare the intruder away. She snatched up a heavy brass lamp, sucked in a determined breath and heaved the lamp through a window in the general direction of the commotion.

The racket that followed made the prior curses

and thumps seem like no more than a mild warm-up. Clearly, the lamp had hit its mark, but the intruder was now mad as hell and very far from being critically injured or terrified. Ashley couldn't quite decide, as she stood there trembling from head to toe, if that was good news or bad.

When the front door was kicked open, she decided it was bad. Instead of scaring the man away, she'd infuriated him. She knew she was no contest for a man in a rage, though the baseball bat did even the odds just a little. Pressed against the wall and out of sight, she clung to the bat with a death grip and cursed the fact that her father had refused to install a phone in the remote cabin.

When silence fell, she realized the intruder was anticipating, just as she was, the next move. She saw no point in wasting time waiting for him to seize the initiative. She wanted to ask how the heck he'd gotten there when she'd never heard a car's engine, but she decided to stick with the basics for now. The phrase know thy enemy came to mind.

She drew in another deep breath, steadied the sturdy bat in her grip, then demanded, "Who's out there?"

The reply was definitely unsuitable for delicate ears and had something to do with her gender. Apparently her unwelcome caller was put out that he'd been bested—so far—by a mere woman.

"Come out with your hands in the air," he commanded in a low, even voice that radiated barely controlled fury.

He sounded like a B-movie hero, she decided,

taking solace in that. The John Waynes and Clint Eastwoods of the world were tougher and more dangerous. They would have burst in, guns blazing, and had her tied to a bedpost by now. The intruder's failure to, well, intrude appeared to give her an edge.

"You don't seem to get it," Ashley retorted with astonishing—or perhaps foolhardy—bravado. "I'm in charge here. You do what I say."

A shot, apparently fired into the air since nothing around her quivering body shattered, decisively countered her claim. This confrontation was definitely not going the way she'd hoped.

"I am dialing 9-1-1 right now," she said in the calmest, most assured tone she could manage with her knees knocking together and no phone within ten miles.

That drew a hoot of disbelieving laughter, which wasn't quite the reaction she'd hoped for.

"Look, lady, you're the interloper here," he declared with surprising conviction. "Once I explain to the cops—assuming you can reach them without a phone line in sight—that you split my head open with..." He hesitated.

"With what?" she demanded with a touch of irony. "A lamp? Hardly a lethal weapon. You're the one firing shots. Is that gun of yours registered, by the way?"

Apparently he saw the problem. He was silent for a full ten seconds.

"But I'm here at the invitation of the owner," he said, trumping her even as he ignored the issue of his gun's legality. "It doesn't take a genius to figure out whose tush is going to get tossed in jail."

The bat wavered in Ashley's hands. This man knew her father? *And* he was bleeding from a wound she'd inflicted with a lamp? Terrific. Her life was on a downhill slide beyond her wildest expectations.

Of course, she only had his word for both the injury and his acquaintance with her father. Trust wasn't exactly her strong suit these days. If her own agent could betray her, who knew what shenanigans this stranger might be up to. She wanted proof.

"Who owns the cabin?" she asked.

"Trent Wilde." He audibly sucked in an apparently painful breath, then added, "Look, sweetheart, it's fun chatting with you, but if I don't get this cut patched up, I'm probably going to bleed to death. Could we call a truce and continue this conversation inside?"

Ashley felt a slight twinge of anxiety and a faint whisper of compassion but steeled herself against both. This guy was beginning to sound legit, but she needed more solid, irrefutable evidence. Knowing her father's name wasn't enough. Everyone in these parts—criminals included, more than likely—knew the cabin belonged to the Wilde family. Trent Wilde had been a powerful figure in Wyoming for years. Few aspects of his life weren't followed in the local media or spread on the energetic gossip hot line. Certainly his real estate acquisitions would have been big news.

"Do you have a key?" she asked. The old lock

was very distinctive. If this man had been in touch with her father, he would have a recognizable key.

"Actually, I thought I'd pick the lock to stay in practice," he snapped.

There was something in his tone that suggested he might very well be experienced enough to do that. Ashley shivered at the thought. It was increasingly possible that she was alone in the wilderness at the mercy of a clever common criminal. Her sense of impending danger escalated another notch.

Unfortunately, it was too late to shut up and run for the hills. She was going to have to brazen it out.

"Just show me the damn key," she ordered. "Toss it in."

With a heavy sigh, he did exactly that. It scooted across the braided rug and landed at her feet. Good aim, she thought grudgingly. Apparently plastering herself against the wall hadn't thrown him off at all. He knew exactly where she was.

She picked the key up as gingerly as if it was a dead scorpion. With its intricately designed head and obvious weight, there was no mistaking the fact it would fit the cabin's lock. She had one just like it in her purse.

"Where did you get it?" she asked suspiciously.

"From the owner," he responded, his exasperation clearly mounting. "Look, we're talking in circles."

"Humor me. Tell me where he is."

"He was in Tucson when I saw him," he said with no hesitation at all. "He's probably in Phoenix now. Or maybe Carefree. How the heck should I know? He's not sitting still for more than a few days at a time. He's a restless man."

Ashley was beginning to get the idea that she'd made a very bad mistake in judgment. Her father was indeed in Arizona, wandering from town to town in search of the perfect retirement village, or so he claimed. *Restless* was an understatement. Trent Wilde had an itch to kick up his heels. No one in the family had dared ask him to define exactly what he meant by that.

Whatever it meant, the family had bets he would be back in Wyoming by fall so he could meddle in their lives at will. He wouldn't be satisfied until he had all three of his daughters married off. So far only Sara had accommodated him, which left Dani and Ashley at the mercy of his devious schemes. For all she knew, this man was part of one of those schemes.

"Okay," she said finally. "Slide your gun in first, then come in very slowly."

A very impressive and very lethal-looking gun scooted to her feet, to precisely the same spot where the key had landed. She was still staring at it in horror when she realized that its owner had entered right along with it, though he'd maintained his distance.

Her gaze cut through the shadows and locked on his well-worn black leather cowboy boots, then traveled slowly up very long, muscular legs clad in black denim. A black T-shirt was tucked into the narrow waistband and fit snugly across a broad chest. A black leather jacket was draped over solid shoulders.

All that unrelenting black—to say nothing of that spine-tinglingly masculine body—triggered an alarm. Once upon a time, there had been a man...well, a boy, really, who'd dressed in that same defiant, daring way. When she finally reached his face, which had a fresh cut just above the left eye, her mouth gaped in recognition and astonishment. Her already jittery nerves set off an adrenaline rush unlike anything she'd felt in years.

"Dillon?" She mouthed the name in little more than a stunned whisper.

His hard mouth quirked into something vaguely resembling a smile. "Hello, sweetheart," he said in a voice as rough and dangerous as bad whiskey and twice as intoxicating. "It's been a long time."

A long time? An eternity was more like it. Ashley could remember every single detail of the last time she had set eyes on Dillon Ford. He'd been running from the law, hightailing it out of town on his beat-up Harley. Or so everyone in town had surmised at the time. They had never cut Dillon much slack, and he'd never been very big on explanations, even when they might have cleared his name.

Judging from the harsh, unrelenting expression on his face right now, he might still be in more trouble than any other ten men combined.

For some reason, though, Ashley was less concerned about that than she was about the fact that even now, after all these years, Dillon Ford still had the ability to make her pulse and her wits scramble.

Despite the unfortunate timing of his arrival, despite this inauspicious beginning, she was ridiculously glad to see him. And that scared her worse than finding a rattler in her bed might have.

Chapter Two

Dillon couldn't help wondering if his blood was pumping so fast because he'd subconsciously guessed that the woman in the cabin was Ashley Wilde. The actual thought had struck him at the precise moment that lamp had shattered a window and grazed his head. It was the kind of outrageous act of which she'd always been capable.

That was what had drawn him to her back in high school. She'd been beautiful, so bright it was scary, and yet there had been an impetuous, daring side to her that had matched his own wild streak. In those days about the only thing the rebellious Dillon Ford hadn't dared was to ask the daughter of Trent Wilde on a date. It was one of his very few regrets.

Moments ago when he had walked through the cabin's front door and seen her, the past ten years had fallen away. A once familiar burst of pure lust had slammed through him, proving once and for all that surging adolescent hormones hadn't been the sole cause of his reaction to her years before.

With his body on high alert, he'd had to work very hard to preserve even a facade of the hard-edged anger that had been all too real only seconds before, with that gash in his head bleeding profusely.

What he really wanted to do was stand silently before her and absorb everything about her, from the clean, crisp scent of her perfume to the porcelain sheen of her skin. He wanted to take his time and examine her from head to toe, from the artfully streaked blond hair and the unusual topaz eyes to those endlessly long, denim-encased legs that were the stuff of very steamy dreams. How had he survived all these years without so much as a glimpse of her?

Of course, that wasn't counting the times he'd stood at a newsstand enthralled by her image on the cover of some glossy fashion magazine. Only the most rigid willpower had prevented him from gathering up all the copies and taking them home with him. Plastering his bedroom walls with her pictures would have seriously interfered with his active love life, a sacrifice he wasn't willing to make for an elusive dream.

His body tightened just looking at her, though with that famed blond hair swept into a bedraggled ponytail and tangled wildly, her heart-shaped face devoid of makeup and her eyes red-rimmed from crying, she wasn't exactly at her best.

Time, it seemed, hadn't dimmed the forbidden attraction he'd felt for her back in the days when he'd been Riverton High's resident juvenile delinquent and she'd been its perennial homecoming queen.

If anything, the lust clamoring through him was more urgent and demanding than ever. The prospect of being locked away with her for a week or two made his jaded heart skip several beats. He'd come to Trent Wilde's cabin to get his bearings. Instead, it appeared he was going to be thrown more off-kilter than ever.

As for Ashley, she was clearly as sassy and arrogant as ever. She had the regal demeanor of a queen...or a woman used to being admired. According to the tabloids, which he'd greedily devoured while waiting in grocery checkout lines, tycoons and royalty had been equally infatuated with her. That alone was enough to make Dillon want to claim her. He wanted her all mussed up and submissive in his bed, the way he'd always believed she was meant to be. Just the thought had him swallowing hard.

Not that her fame didn't have its dark side. Though he doubted she was aware of it, he knew all about the obsessed fan who'd threatened her for a few months the year before. She'd hired a Los Angeles security company for protection. His company. It had taken an act of supreme restraint to keep from claiming the assignment for himself. He'd known he could never be as objective as the case required.

But, oh, how he had longed to see her again. Finding her here was better than any fantasy he could have contrived.

Before he knew what he intended, before he could consider the consequences, he'd taken a step closer. Acting on pure impulse, he reached out and hauled her into his arms.

Surprise worked in his favor. His mouth slanted across hers just the way he'd always envisioned kissing her, softly, gently, but with so much restrained passion he ached with it.

She fit perfectly, snugly against him. Her mouth molded to his with surprising willingness. The spring night might be rainy and bone-deep cold, but the heat that erupted inside him could have burned the whole damn state to the ground.

Years of pent-up hunger went into that kiss. Years of practice on poor substitutes gave it a finesse that had both of them breathing hard in a heartbeat. He was left with a sense of wonder that an act so familiar could seem so fresh, so rare, so damned dangerous.

When he released her at last, there was a dazed expression on her face and pure fire in her eyes. She might have kissed him eagerly, but now her open hand connected with his cheek with a force that snapped his head back.

Dillon grinned approvingly. He'd expected as much from the quick-tempered Ashley he recalled. She never had wanted to admit just how badly she wanted him. That kiss, however, had spoken volumes.

"Still feisty, I see," he commented.

Fire blazed in her eyes. "And you are every bit as rude and obnoxious and low-class as you always were."

His smile widened. "Still a bit of a snob, too."

Color flamed in her cheeks. "I'm surprised you're not in jail by now," she countered with feeling.

"You and everyone else in town," he said dryly. "Sorry to disappoint you."

"I'm not disappointed," she claimed. "Just surprised. Now would you mind telling me what the hell you're doing with a key to my father's cabin?"

He shook his head with exaggerated dismay. "I thought we covered that. You used to be much quicker. Straight A's, as I recall."

Hands on hips, she glared at him. "I mean it, Dillon. I want to know how you got that key. You've got five seconds or I call the sheriff."

Though the answer was simple enough, she was having so much fun thinking he was here illegally, he couldn't help taunting her.

He glanced deliberately around the cabin for some sign of that phone she was threatening to use. He knew perfectly well, as she did, that there wasn't one. Trent had craved the isolation the cabin afforded him. He'd refused to have one installed, which was one reason his daughters almost never came here, he'd claimed. Not a one of them could stay off the phone for more than a minute at a time, he'd said with a father's typical bemusement.

Apparently he'd been wrong about one daughter, Dillon thought. Which meant a distinct change in his own plans for the next week or two. He, too, had wanted to get away from the demands of the real world for a while. He'd wanted to be cut off completely from a life that had lately become too complicated and far too structured to suit him. He couldn't seem to dredge up much disappointment at the change in plans.

"And how would you be planning to reach the sheriff?" he inquired.

"Ever heard of cell phones?"

"Of course," he said readily. "Every self-respecting thief has one."

"I'm sure you'd know all about that, wouldn't you?"

Dillon had been reformed for a long time now. He'd been a respected businessman for most of that time. It should have infuriated him to have everything he'd worked so hard to achieve stripped away with one disparaging remark from a woman who didn't know him at all anymore.

Instead, though, he suddenly felt like the town's bad boy all over again, and he loved it. The danger and excitement he'd been craving rushed through him. Respectability apparently hadn't satisfied him as much as he thought it had.

Damn, but it was good to be home. It was even better being locked away in the wilderness with the woman who'd made his blood run hot since the very first day he'd laid eyes on her. This time, he vowed, he was going to discover what it was like to make her his own.

Then and now, Dillon Ford was the most exasperating, most troublesome man Ashley could ever recall having the misfortune of knowing. He was incapable of giving a straight answer and more inclined to lie than tell the truth.

In high school, his heated, knowing looks had set off forbidden yearnings deep inside her. Not once, though, had he ever acted on the dangerous promise that was there in his eyes every time his gaze caught hers. The gulf between them had been as wide and deep as any ocean on the planet.

She had dated the football captains and the class presidents, flirted outrageously with baseball heroes and the sons of the town's wealthiest citizens. Hardly a tongue-tied boy in her high school class hadn't stumbled over his own feet in her presence. All of them…except Dillon Ford. It had been exasperating. Naturally that made him the one she wanted, the one she found most intriguing.

Older than she was by three years—an eternity at that age—Dillon had never been shy. He had dated the girls whose reputations were in tatters by the time they turned fifteen. He'd flaunted his sexuality in a way that left girls breathless in his presence and parents terrified. Dani, who was in his class, had talked about him in whispers, which had promptly piqued Ashley's curiosity.

Ashley had always known that if she and Dillon had so much as spoken in the school corridor, tongues would have wagged for a month. But, oh, how she had been tempted to do more than just speak to him! She'd flirted more than once with the idea of messing up her spit-and-polish, good-girl image once and for all. Dillon could have accomplished that with no more than a wink, but he'd never cooperated, quashing her rebellion before it could ever really flower. Apparently, he enjoyed taunting her, but not enough to waste time on a Goody Two-shoes, when far more experienced girls were at his beck and call.

Just once had they crossed the line, and even then it had been at Ashley's instigation, not Dillon's. At his senior prom, which she'd attended with the Harvard-bound son of her father's closest friend, she had found herself standing next to Dillon by the punch bowl. She'd been surprised he'd chosen to come at all, but apparently even the class rebel couldn't stay away from such a momentous event.

Flying in the face of common sense, she had boldly asked him to dance. She'd been tempted for too long to resist the chance to discover what it felt like to be held in those muscular arms. Amusement glinting in his eyes at her daring, he had led her onto the dance floor.

The oh-so-slow dance had started with a proper distance between them. But, as if drawn by a magnet, Ashley had moved closer and closer until her head was tucked on his shoulder. She had sighed with incomparable contentment.

Even now, she shivered at the memory of feminine awareness she had discovered that night. Flirting had never excited her as Dillon's dark-eyed gaze had. Stolen kisses were nothing compared to the whisper-light touch of his hand on her back. No boy's most daring caress had thrilled her the way the brush of Dillon's thighs against her own had.

It was just because he was forbidden, because he was so bad that no decent girl would date him, she had told herself that night. Now, with his gaze hot on her once again and her body trembling like a schoolgirl's in response, she wondered if it was more than that. Or was she more than ever trying to rebel against a lifetime of being everyone's perfect little good girl?

Whatever the case, she had to get him out of the cabin and she had to do it now, before he felled her senses with another one of those unexpected, staggering kisses. Her life was messed up enough without succumbing to a ridiculous urge to jump into the sack with Dillon Ford. She assured herself that she was past a need to rebel, way past.

Wasn't she?

She skimmed a quick glance over dark hair that had a distinct curl to it, lingered on a scowling but astonishingly tempting mouth, then dared a peek at black eyes so intense they sent a once familiar tremble through her. Maybe she wasn't as safe from those old urges as she'd thought.

She'd recalled Dillon more than once over the past ten years. In fact, Sara had taunted her about him only a few months ago, stirring old fantasies to life. Sara had encouraged her to seek out someone like Dillon, who would shake up her predictable existence. Little had they known....

But the truth was her memory and her wildest fantasies hadn't done him justice. He was more gorgeous, more thoroughly masculine, more down-and-dirty real than the sexiest male models she'd worked with through the years.

Before she could figure out a reasonably polite way to send him out into the rain, he retrieved his gun, tucked it into the waistband of his jeans and gestured toward the visible kitchen area. Clearly he intended to make himself thoroughly at home.

"Any coffee made?"

The mundane question snapped her back to reality. She nodded.

"It should still be hot," she said as she crossed the room, grateful for the chance to put some distance between them.

She injected a briskly polite note into her voice. "If you'd like to change out of those wet clothes before you leave, I'll pour you a cup for the road. And there are plenty of first-aid supplies in the bathroom, if you want to bandage that cut."

He grinned in a thoroughly male, tolerant way that suggested he found her less than subtle approach amusing.

"There's enough heat in here to dry my clothes in no time," he said. "As for the cut, you could always kiss it and make it better."

She scowled at his teasing. "Not too long ago you were claiming you were likely to bleed to death from that wound," she reminded him.

"A ploy," he admitted unrepentantly.

"For sympathy? I doubt it."

"No, to get inside. Worked, too," he said.

He made the claim with so much arrogance, it was all Ashley could do to keep from dumping the cup of hot coffee into his lap. Instead, she handed it to him gingerly, careful to avoid so much as grazing his knuckles. His amused expression proved he knew exactly how thoroughly he'd disconcerted her with that kiss.

"This should wake you up so you'll be alert for the drive back to town," she said pointedly. "You should be back in plenty of time to get a room at the hotel and still catch a good night's sleep."

The comment drew a grin, but no retort.

She sat on the edge of the chair across from him and watched as he sipped the coffee, practically counting the minutes until he would be out of the cabin and a good, safe distance away from her life.

"I came up here to fish and I'm not going anywhere, you know," he said after a while.

The direct challenge had her gritting her teeth. "Yes," she said just as emphatically, "you are. Besides, as I can attest firsthand, the fish aren't biting. It'll be a waste of your time."

"It's the process, not the results that count," he said lazily. "I'll be happy enough just to wade into the stream and toss my line in."

"Oh, sure. I've always thought of you as the laid-back type," she commented sarcastically.

He got up, strolled into the kitchen and poured himself another cup of coffee, probably just to irritate her with his deliberate nonchalance.

It worked, too. She really, really wanted to slug him for the second time in less than an hour. It was an urge she had never, ever experienced before, much less acted on.

"Did your father know you were coming up here?" he asked when he returned to the living room.

"No," she admitted. Sighing, she prepared for another round of sparring.

"And he obviously loaned me the cabin," he pointed out with annoying logic, waving that damnable key under her nose again. "How do you think he'd feel about you tossing me out?"

"He sure as hell wouldn't want us both here at the same time," Ashley said, though she wasn't nearly as sure of that as she wanted to be. Her father was pretty desperate to marry her off to just about anyone.

"Tsk, tsk, where are your manners?" Dillon retorted, clearly unoffended by her derogatory tone. "You shouldn't be judging a guest in your home."

"You are not my guest," she repeated emphatically.

"Exactly. I'm your father's guest, which means you should be treating me with kindness and respect," he said triumphantly. "Isn't that the way you were brought up?"

Ashley practically groaned aloud. Of course, that was the way she'd been brought up, and Dillon knew it. He'd presented her with the heart of her dilemma—good manners versus a panicky desire to be rid of him.

Their battle over who had claim to the cabin seemed destined to go on forever. Ashley's head throbbed like the dickens, but she wasn't about to yield the point by going off to bed with the issue unresolved.

She rallied half a dozen more arguments, but Dillon clearly wasn't budging. Short of dragging him bodily out the door, which she doubted she could have managed anyway, she was fresh out of alternatives. Sometime after midnight, she grudgingly threw in the towel.

"Oh, for heaven's sake, just sleep here tonight," she finally muttered, as if conceding him a great favor. "I'm too exhausted to keep arguing about it. You'll find towels in the closet in the bathroom and a guest room at the end of the hall. Don't expect me to make the bed for you. I'm sure you can manage on your own."

"Where beds are concerned, I'm an expert," he said.

"I'm sure," she acknowledged as images flooded her mind and color flooded her cheeks.

"And I know where things are in the cabin. You don't need to worry about me."

Surprised by his claim to be familiar with the cabin, Ashley stared hard at him. "How? Have you broken in before?"

He waved the key under her nose...again. "It's not breaking and entering when you have the owner's permission," he repeated with exaggerated patience. "It's not the first time I've been here, sweetheart. I'm probably more familiar with this place than you are. When was the last time you stole away here for a little solitude?"

He had her there. "Never, but that's beside the

point,'' she said airily. ''How do you know so much about the cabin?''

''I've come here to fish with your father a time or two. Came back last year on my own, when I needed a break.''

''A break from what?''

''This and that,'' he said unhelpfully.

''And my father gave you the key just like that?''

''Just like that,'' he agreed. ''He popped it into overnight mail the minute we got off the phone.''

She stared at him, bemused by what he was suggesting. ''Are you suggesting that you and my father are buddies?''

''Do you have a problem with that?''

''Actually, the very thought boggles the mind,'' she said, unconcerned about offending him. Clearly his ego was strong enough to take anything she cared to dish out.

He grinned, in fact. ''No more than the thought of you and me, sweetheart. And just look at the two of us all alone together here in the wilderness.''

The words sent a shiver chasing down her spine. That old promise was in his eyes again, along with a bit of a dare. Ashley figured she better get out of the room before she took him up on it.

''Good night,'' she said hurriedly and headed down the hall.

''Sweet dreams,'' he called softly after her.

Sweet? Hell, if she was very, very lucky, any dreams she had tonight wouldn't burn the house down.

Chapter Three

Alone in the master bedroom, in the middle of the suddenly enormous and seductive feather mattress, Ashley determinedly closed her eyes and tried to shut out all thoughts of the impossible man who'd invaded her privacy. It was like trying to plug a hole in the Hoover Dam with a wad of gum.

If she hadn't been certain her father had no way of knowing she was at the cabin, she would have suspected him of setting her up. It would be just like him to put a macho, egotistical, testosterone-laden bully in her path just so he could sit back and watch the fireworks.

But Dillon Ford? Was her father that perverse?

Yes, of course, he was. He'd been telling her for the past ten years that the only men she was likely to meet in New York were criminals and wimps. Of course, that was his opinion of anyone who would knowingly choose to live crammed together in itty-bitty apartments, instead of on their own several-thousand-acre spread.

She had a feeling there was a fascinating story behind any friendship that had blossomed between Dillon and her father. Maybe before she kicked him out in the morning, she'd ask Dillon for the details.

More than likely, though, Dillon was on the run from the law, and Trent Wilde, exercising his own brand of justice, was choosing to help him hide out.

Or maybe...oh, what the heck, the possibilities were endless. She'd never in a million years guess the truth. Her father's thought processes were too unpredictable, except when it came to scheming to marry off his daughters.

By daybreak she was exhausted, irritable and more determined than ever to get Dillon out of the cabin. She claimed she couldn't wait to be rid of him. However, she dressed more carefully than she had since her arrival. She took her time brushing her hair until it gleamed, added a light dusting of makeup, steeled herself for battle and then stormed into the living room.

Since she was prepared for all-out verbal warfare, Dillon, naturally, was nowhere to be found. A quick fizz of relief was all too rapidly dispelled by a vague sense of disappointment. Their verbal gymnastics—or whatever, she thought dryly—the night before had kicked her adrenaline into gear. Apparently she'd been hoping for more of the same. For reasons it was probably best not to examine too closely, she'd felt more alive in those few hours than she had in a long, long time.

Better, though, that he was gone, she decided as she poured herself a cup of the rich, caffeine-laden coffee he'd brewed. She needed serenity right now far more than she needed a little sexual tension or a masculine sparring partner.

She'd wasted days on self-pity. It was time to start making plans for her life. Logical, sensible plans. Plans that most definitely did not include a fling with a man of Dillon Ford's questionable reputation and penchant for heartbreaking. Ninety-nine percent of the women in Riverton under the age of thirty could probably testify that he was bad news. She certainly didn't want to be the one to give him a perfect record.

Satisfied that she was on the verge of taking control of her destiny again, she sank into a comfortable chair and tucked her feet under her. Just as she prepared to get on with some serious thinking, she heard an all-too-familiar thump on the front deck. She closed her eyes and sighed. Apparently she'd spoken too soon. Trouble was back on the horizon. To her very deep regret, anticipation kicked in with predictable urgency.

When Dillon entered a moment later, carrying two fat, sparkling trout, she could cheerfully have shot all three of them.

Where the dickens had those fish been, when she'd been standing hip-deep in the water for the past week? The fact that she'd informed Dillon the night before that the fish weren't biting made his gloating expression all the harder to take.

"I thought you weren't all that interested in actually reeling in a fish," she commented, ignoring the laudable size of his catch. "Or did you go out this morning just to prove that I was wrong and that you—the superior male of the species—could lure one in?"

"Why would I need to prove anything to you?" he inquired in a testy way that suggested she'd hit the nail on the head.

"You're a man, aren't you?"

Ignoring the jibe, he wrapped the fish, stuck them in the refrigerator, then returned to settle in the chair opposite her, coffee mug in hand. Once again, he looked as if he had no intention of budging. She had to admit, he looked more at home in her father's very masculine wood and leather environment than she did. That grated on her nerves, too. Wasn't there anywhere these days that she belonged?

"Maybe we should talk about this attitude you seem to have toward men," Dillon suggested helpfully.

That was a path Ashley had no intention of going down. Men were a topic she'd avoided ever since her last disastrous relationship. She'd discovered that Linc, like so many others infatuated with the glamour of modeling, had wanted a trophy, not a woman. Now that her modeling career was in doubt, she suspected her suitors would be moving on to new cover girls.

"There's no time to discuss my attitudes or anything else," she said blithely.

"Oh, are you going somewhere?"

"Nope, but you are. While you were gone, I gave this a lot of thought. I'll make a couple of calls. I'm sure one of my father's friends would be happy to loan you another cabin. In fact, there's one about fifty miles upstream I'm sure would be available."

He grinned. "Fifty miles, huh? Do I make you that nervous?"

"Oh, go to hell."

"I wish I could accommodate you, but I like it here."

"I was here first," she reminded him, then clamped her mouth shut. This conversation was promising to disintegrate just as rapidly as the one they'd had the night before. Another argument would resolve nothing. It would just add to his impression that she was scared of being close to him. The sky would turn green before she'd admit that.

He shrugged. "It's not as if this is some tiny little shack. We'll share. If we work hard at it, we'll hardly notice each other."

Despite her resolve to find a workable compromise, Ashley was shaking her head before he'd finished. "No way. I came here for solitude, so I could do some thinking."

"Do you have a lot on your mind?" he asked, his gaze all too penetrating.

"Don't we all?" she retorted.

"Maybe you need to do your thinking aloud to an objective outsider."

"And that would be you?"

"Naturally."

"No, thanks. If I want an outsider's opinion, I'll see a shrink."

"I'm cheaper and I'm here."

"Yes, but you're rapidly becoming part of the problem."

He grinned. "Already? We're just getting reacquainted."

"Some people are just born nuisances."

"You look as if your life could use a little shaking up," he retorted.

The comment was more accurate than she might have liked. What she really needed, though, was time alone to figure out what she was going to do with herself if her modeling career was over. Fortunately, she had more than enough money to take her time deciding. What she didn't have at the moment was the solitude she craved.

"By the way, I noticed this morning that you're a little short on groceries," Dillon said. "Maybe we should take a drive to the market and pick up a few things. All this fresh air gives me an appetite. What about you?"

Unfortunately, her appetite was flourishing, too. She'd staved off disaster by stocking only the bare essentials, a little soup, some fresh fruit, a mountain of vegetables. She'd worked her way through most of them the first few days, eating compulsively to satisfy a hunger that clearly wasn't entirely physical. The thought of a grocery store, its shelves lined with temptation, made her mouth water.

"If you're not happy with what's here, you go," she said determinedly. "I have everything I need right here."

"There were three oranges and a pear, when I checked."

"That'll do for today," she said stubbornly. "And we do have those fish you caught."

He studied her so intently, she felt herself blushing.

"You mean that, don't you?" he said at last.

It had cost her the last of her willpower to get the words out, but she would never in a million years admit that to him. "Yes," she said instead.

"What happens if I decide to claim half, say one orange and the pear, along with my share of the fish?"

"I'd have to break your arm," Ashley said grimly.

Dillon chuckled, then fell silent when she didn't even smile. "You mean that, too, don't you?"

"Try me."

"I don't think so. I'll go to the market by myself. You may have the appetite of a bird, but I don't. I need junk food and meat to survive."

His words set off warning bells. "Junk food? Meat?"

"Sure. Potato chips, tortilla chips and salsa, beer. Some hamburger. A big, thick steak. The stuff that makes life worth living."

Sighing heavily, Ashley stood up. "Maybe I'd better go with you, after all."

"What's the matter? Don't you approve of my menu?"

The trouble was she craved it all. "That stuff will kill you," she retorted.

"Not in moderation."

"When did you ever do anything in moderation?"

"Okay, you have a point," he conceded. "Maybe I could use some guidance. I'll get my keys and we'll go."

The mention of his keys reminded her that she'd never heard his car the night before. "How did you get here, anyway? I never heard an engine."

"You must not have been listening too closely, then. I assure you I didn't walk up here." He stroked a finger down her cheek as he passed. "I'll be with you in a minute, sweetheart."

Ashley practically ran outside, hoping for a blast of Arctic air to cool off her flushed skin. Unfortunately, spring was back, and the warm air was filled with promise. The rain had given way to bright blue skies. It was the kind of day that made sap and hormones run wild.

She scanned the driveway for a second car but spotted none, which renewed her questions about Dillon's mode of transportation. When he walked out and headed toward the edge of the woods, she automatically fell into step behind him.

A few seconds later, her gaze fell on an impressive motorcycle. Black, naturally. If memory served, it was the same one Dillon had ridden out of town on years before. She was amazed he hadn't had to hock it long before now.

"You expect me to ride on that?" she demanded.

He grinned. "You know you always wanted to."

"Did not," she said, even as she moved toward it with an eagerness that belied the words. Riding on this Harley, her arms wrapped around Dillon's waist as the wind whipped through her hair, had represented the epitome of excitement and rebellion as far back as she could recall.

He halted and appeared to waver. "Would you rather go in your car?" he asked, his expression innocent.

"Oh, for heaven's sake, let's just go," she said huffily, climbing onto the motorcycle.

Dillon grinned as he swung his leg over the seat and settled in front of her. "You ever been on one of these?"

"Never."

He warned her to lean with him, not against him on the curves. "And hang on tight," he added.

The last was unnecessary. As soon as he'd fired up the engine, Ashley circled his waist with her arms and clung.

For the first hundred yards or so, she closed her eyes against a wave of pure terror. When no bolt of lightning struck as punishment for her decision to climb on the Harley, and when they didn't land in a ditch straight off, she dared to open her eyes again.

The rush of wind caught at her hair and tugged it loose from its neat ponytail. Dillon's sharp masculine scent was mixed with the freshness of outdoors to tease at her senses. His vibrant energy and excitement tugged at her, surrounded her just as his warmth seemed to. The whole effect was...exhilarating, wonderfully, disturbingly exhilarating.

Old fantasies merged with reality. This was Dillon, every shockingly sensual inch of him. Her fingers were linked across his flat belly. Her breasts brushed against his back. Suddenly, heart-stoppingly aware of every provocative sway of their bodies together, Ashley felt like laughing with pure joy at the thrill of it all.

Though she wasn't aware of any sound actually emerging, she must have laughed aloud, because Dillon joined her. He slanted a quick, thoroughly devilish look over his shoulder and winked.

He said something that sounded vaguely like, "Told you so," though the wind caught snatches of the words and carried them away.

He couldn't have ruined her mood with his taunts if he'd tried. For the second time in less than twenty-four hours, Ashley felt alive again. For once she decided against questioning the cause of this unexpected happiness. For the next few hours or days, she would stop fighting the inevitable. She would simply accept that Dillon had brought something into her life that had been missing.

And for now, that was enough.

Grocery shopping with Ashley was an experience in pure frustration, Dillon decided as they roamed the overflowing aisles of the small country market.

For one thing, there was the sway of her hips as she sashayed ahead of him around pyramids of canned goods and bins of fruit. If that motorcycle ride hadn't already sent his hormones off the charts, watching her cute little tush would have done the job.

Aside from trying to keep his rampaging lust under control, there was also the little problem of actually getting something he considered edible into their basket. She balked at potato chips. They had an outright row over tortilla chips. They finally settled for pretzels. No-fat pretzels.

He supposed this obsession she had over the fat content of every little bitty item he plucked off the shelves had something to do with her career, but it was darned annoying all the same. He didn't think there was anything wrong with her body just as it was. In fact, a few more pounds wouldn't hurt. It would soften some of those sharp angles that might look great in a photograph, but didn't look especially cuddly in real life.

Not that he was complaining. He'd want to cuddle Ashley even if she looked like a damned stick. The truth of that had never been more apparent to him than it had become in the past twenty-four hours. No adolescent had ever been in a more constant state of aching arousal than he appeared to be in.

He paused beside a crate of potatoes, envisioning them smothered with butter and sour cream or maybe mashed and swimming in gravy. He tossed a few into the basket, mindful that they could manage only so much on the Harley. For once Ashley didn't even blink an eye.

Unfortunately when they came to the dairy case, she smacked his hand as he reached for the butter and selected a container of no-fat sour cream that had him grinding his teeth. The instant her back was turned, he grabbed the butter. Two glorious pounds of it.

"I saw that," she sang over her shoulder. "Put it back."

"Not a chance, sweetheart. I probably should have taken a stand over the chips, but I didn't. I'm taking one now. If I want butter, then I'll have butter. And meat," he added, grabbing a handful of steaks.

"All that stuff will clog your arteries," she countered. "You'll be dead before you hit fifty."

"That's a chance I'm willing to take." He peered straight into her eyes and said seriously, "Sweetheart, at some point, you have to decide which things make life worth living."

Her disapproving expression faded. Her lips began to quirk up at the corners. "And for you that's butter and beef?"

"Among other things," he said with a deliberately provocative note in his voice.

Ashley promptly blushed and looked away.

"That, too," he said, chuckling, "but actually I was referring to food."

"Sure you were."

"I swear it." He crossed his heart to prove it. "Fudge brownies, for instance. Rocky Road ice cream. Big, juicy hamburgers with crisp onion rings."

She rolled her eyes at the litany. "As if I'd believe anything you swore to."

"Still misjudging me," he said with exaggerated sorrow. "And after we've been so close."

The shocked gasp he heard had not come from Ashley. He turned slowly and spotted a short, gray-haired woman in baggy denims, an even baggier sweatshirt and bright red high-top sneakers. She had disapproval written all over her pinched face.

Dillon might not have recognized the casual, ill-fitting outfit, but he would have recognized that face anywhere. He'd stared at it every morning for his third period algebra class his sophomore year. And again his junior year, when he'd had to repeat the class.

"Why, hello, there, Mrs. Fawcett," he said cheerfully. Despite her current expression, she was the one teacher at Riverton High he remembered with any degree of fondness. She might have flunked him, but she'd eventually bullied him into learning.

"Dillon Ford, you are as incorrigible as ever," she announced in the same voice she would have used to dismiss a pesky student. Her gaze shifted to Ashley. "As for you, I'm shocked to find you with this..."

Words seemed to fail her. She finally settled for calling him a mischief-maker. Dillon hid a chuckle at her notion of a disparaging label. She had had a whole list of names she'd trotted out years ago when she'd been displeased with his performance in class. Apparently she'd forgotten them.

"I'm not with him," Ashley said in a rush. "That is...oh, never mind. It's good to see you, Mrs. Fawcett. Dani wrote to me about your retirement. How have you been enjoying all your free time?"

"I'm bored stiff," she said succinctly.

Dillon watched as a spark of pure devilment lit Ashley's eyes.

"Perhaps you'd enjoy a ride on Dillon's motorcycle, then," she suggested to their old teacher. "It's remarkable how young and alive it makes you feel."

Delighted with Ashley's probably unintended admission that she had enjoyed the ride, Dillon was quick to jump in and echo the invitation. "Come on, Mrs. Fawcett. How about a quick spin, just to the top of the hill and back?"

"Young man, I will not be climbing on the back of that contraption in this lifetime," she said, despite a rather wistful glance outside at the offensive vehicle.

She scowled at Ashley. "And you have no business on it, either. It's improper and dangerous. You, of all people, should understand how important it is not to give others the wrong impression. Why, you were the most responsible, well-behaved girl I ever taught. It was no surprise to me that you went off and became a big success. I always knew you'd accomplish anything you set your mind to."

To Dillon's amazement, Ashley looked thoroughly uncomfortable at the lavish praise. Rather than basking in it as her due, she looked as if she wished she was someplace else. Before he could figure out the meaning of her odd reaction, he caught Mrs. Fawcett's wistful glance straying to the motorcycle again.

He couldn't let a moment like this pass. He leaned down. "Dare you."

Color flamed in her overly powdered cheeks. "Never," she insisted with a huff.

"Never's a very long time," he taunted. "Isn't it time you did something totally unpredictable?"

"I do not need to take foolish risks. Nor do I need to prove anything to you, young man."

"It's perfectly safe," Ashley chimed in. "Dillon's a very skilled driver."

"He's certainly been at it long enough," the teacher said. She glared at him. "Isn't it time you grew up and started driving a real car? Perhaps a nice, safe sedan?"

Dillon thought of the fleet of "real" cars he had in his garage in California, including a stretch limo that was so dull and safe he refused to use it except on those occasions that demanded he make a show of his success. There were people in Los Angeles who wouldn't hire his security company unless they thought he was their social equal. He had to make it seem that hiring Security-Wise was a status symbol.

"I have a real car," he conceded. "I save the motorcycle for special occasions back here in Wyoming. I'd hate to disappoint the good folks of Riverton by turning into another average, straight-arrow guy. You all have always counted on me to be the town bad boy. You really would die of boredom if I took that away from you."

"Some of us had higher expectations for you," Mrs. Fawcett chided. "The only thing that disappoints me, young man, is when someone fails to live up to his true potential. Perhaps it's time you thought about that."

That said, she whirled around and marched out of the store, her back ramrod straight, her shoulders set rigidly.

When she was gone, Dillon faced Ashley and caught her trying unsuccessfully to hide a smile.

"I guess she told you," she said.

"Care to make a wager?" Dillon asked.

"What kind of wager?"

"Five bucks says I get her on the motorcycle before I leave town."

"No way. You heard her. She will not take foolish risks."

"Five bucks," he repeated.

Ashley grinned. "Easy money. You're on."

Since he appeared to be on a roll, he decided to up the ante. "Want to make another wager?"

She hesitated and regarded him suspiciously. "On?"

"Whether or not you and I will be able to stay in the same house for the next week or so without making love."

He saw his mistake the instant the words left his lips. He'd put her on notice about his intentions. Ashley was far too stubborn to let him win that kind of a bet. In fact, she looked mad enough to bop him over the head with that giant zucchini she was holding. At least, they both knew exactly where they stood now.

"That one's a foregone conclusion," she snapped. "You can hand over the money now, because the odds of you and me getting involved are about the same as those of Prince Charles and Di reconciling."

Dillon's pulse hummed. Let her dig in her heels. He loved a good challenge. That would make his victory all the sweeter.

Already planning for the eventual outcome, he grabbed a bottle of outrageously expensive champagne and tossed it into the cart. The gesture drew a scowl.

"Planning a party?" she inquired testily.

"A celebration."

It was obvious to him from her chilly expression that she knew exactly what he was saying.

"The only celebrating going on at that cabin will be on the day you leave," she said.

Dillon heaved an exaggerated sigh. "Sweetheart, you're breaking my heart."

"I doubt you have one."

He reached out and tucked a finger under her chin and forced her to meet his gaze. "If that's true, Ashley Wilde, it's because you stole it years ago."

Chapter Four

How could Dillon say something chauvinistically male and outrageous one minute and something so sweet and romantic the next? Ashley wondered during the ride to the cabin. One minute she had wanted to smack him for practically daring her to sleep with him, and the next he'd accused her of stealing his heart years ago.

Which Dillon Ford was she supposed to trust? Probably neither one of them, when it came right down to it. For all she knew Dillon was a master of manipulation who knew exactly what he was doing when he'd melted her heart with that remark about her effect on him. It had probably been the first step in his deliberate campaign to get what he wanted—her in his bed. That wager of his might only be for a few bucks, but he clearly took it seriously.

She spent the rest of the day giving him a wide berth, but there was no way to avoid him over dinner. While she'd been off on a solitary walk, he'd grilled the fish on her father's gas barbecue, created some sort of vegetable and rice concoction that looked better than anything she knew how to prepare, and warmed a loaf of sourdough bread, which he actually claimed to have baked from scratch. Since no such loaf had been in with their groceries, she had to believe him.

He'd set the table on the deck. "It's too nice a night to eat indoors," he said as she approached. "Is this okay?"

"It's fine with me. It's cooling off, now that the sun's going down. Let me get a sweater."

He gestured toward the back of a chair. "I brought one out for you."

The thought of Dillon in her room, going through her things, had her swallowing hard. It seemed there were limits to the degree of intimacy she was prepared to accept.

She was about to lambast him for invading her private space when he said mildly, "It was in the living room, in case you're worrying that I was going through your stuff."

His ability to see straight through her startled her. She must be far more transparent than she'd been led to believe. All those years of practice at hiding her real emotions in front of a camera hadn't paid off, after all. Now, when it really counted, she couldn't seem to mask a thing.

"Thanks," she said, pulling the warm crewneck

sweater on over her T-shirt. She sat gingerly across from him. "Everything smells wonderful. Where'd you learn to cook?"

"You seem to have forgotten my background," he said.

Ashley immediately recalled the forgotten tales of his childhood—a mother who'd died when he was a boy, a father who traveled on business. More often than not, Dillon had been left to manage for himself and his younger brother and sister. It was no wonder, everyone had said at the time, that he'd run wild. There'd been no discipline or parental supervision at home.

"I'm sorry," she said. "I'd forgotten how difficult times must have been for you back then."

He shrugged. "We got along. I learned my way around a kitchen in a hurry. Actually, I enjoy cooking. It seems to be the only creative task at which I excel. Can't sing worth a darn. Can't dance or draw." He grinned. "Obviously, I couldn't do algebra. Took me two years to pass the class."

"Algebra wasn't creative," Ashley countered. "It was drudgery."

"How can you say that? You were in an advanced class and you got an A in that."

She stared at him in surprise. "You remember all that?"

"When you were as bad as I was in a subject, you knew exactly which students were acing it. Did you know Mrs. Fawcett wanted to arrange for you to tutor me?"

"Really?" she said in amazement. "Why didn't she?"

"I wouldn't let her. I couldn't have afforded to pay you. More than that, though, I didn't want you to see how lousy I was. I had my tender, male pride at stake. You were two years behind me, after all."

"I think Mrs. Fawcett is actually very fond of you," Ashley said.

"Oh, really," he said doubtfully. "Is that why she looked so horrified when she saw the two of us together today?"

"That was because she now knows the juiciest piece of gossip in all of Wyoming and she can't share it," Ashley said. "Thank goodness, she's always disapproved of spreading rumors."

"Worried about your reputation?" Dillon asked with a faint note of defensiveness.

"Of course not," Ashley said without the slightest hesitation. "I came here to do some thinking. If my sisters hear that I'm at Daddy's cabin, they'll be up here pestering me to know why I'm hiding out."

"That's the second time you've said something about needing solitude to think. Are you sure you don't want to talk with an objective observer about whatever's on your mind? I'm not sure I'd recommend listening to any advice I dole out, but I can be a decent sounding board."

Ashley shook her head. "Thanks, but I have to work this through on my own. Now let's get back to you. What other subjects did you struggle with in high school?"

The past struck her as safer ground than the present, perhaps for both of them. She had no idea what Dillon's life was like these days, and for the moment it seemed like a very good idea to keep it that way. She wasn't sure she was prepared to handle the news that he was one step away from being carted off to jail.

"All of them," he said, apparently accepting her reluctance to talk about her own problems. "I wasn't much of a student. I was too easily distracted, especially in high school." He sighed dramatically. "All those girls and so little time."

"Exactly how many did you make a pass at?"

His expression sobered. "All of them except you, I suppose."

Ashley couldn't decide whether to be hurt by the admission or incensed by it, even though she'd guessed as much long ago. "Why'd you leave me out?"

To her surprise he looked as if the question made him uncomfortable. "Dillon?" she prodded.

"You were different."

"A snob?" she asked, thinking of a remark he'd made the night before. It had brought back similar accusations from the other boys she'd kept at arm's distance then.

None of them had understood that staying focused on her goal of getting away from Riverton had been paramount. She'd refused to let her feelings for anyone interfere with that. She could see, now, how that might have been misinterpreted by fragile young male egos. Dillon's ego, however, had hardly been fragile.

"No," he said at once, confirming that his ego had never been shattered. Nor had he feared rejection, apparently. His warm gaze met hers and held. "You were special, too good for the likes of me."

"Oh." It was the last thing she had expected him to say.

He grinned. "You sound surprised. Surely I'm not the first man ever to tell you how special you are."

"Maybe you're just the first one who ever sounded like he really meant it," she said candidly.

"I do mean it," he said emphatically. Then, his expression thoughtful, he added, "I suppose you've met some creeps and jerks in your business, though."

"More than a few."

She toyed with her rice, trying to figure out how to explain so that he would understand. Linc had been a perfect example of the problem. She used him to characterize the type of man she tended to meet.

"The problem with most of them isn't that they're awful people," she explained. "It's just that they never really see *me*. They see the face or the figure and never look any deeper than that. Sometimes I wonder..." Her voice trailed off as she realized she was opening the very topic she had just moments earlier sworn to avoid.

"Wonder what?"

Because he sounded genuinely interested and because deep down she did need someone to really listen, she tried to explain at least some of what she was feeling.

"Sometimes I wonder if even I know who I am anymore," she admitted with a trace of wistfulness in her voice.

He didn't laugh at the statement or remind her that she was Trent Wilde's daughter and a famous model. Instead, he simply asked, "How so?"

He sounded so eager to understand that she told him.

"The modeling business demands that you project an image, that you represent glamour and beauty. It doesn't demand that you have an idea in your head or care whether you woke up with the flu. Pretty soon you learn to shut all those other things out so you can do the job. Then one day you wake up and worry that maybe there's nothing left inside anymore."

He nodded his understanding. "So, is that why you're here?"

"Part of it."

"And the other part?"

As kind as Dillon was being, Ashley wasn't about to tell him she'd been bounced from her job because she was too fat. No one who wasn't as obsessed with looks as a model could possibly understand why a few pounds mattered so desperately. Nor did she want to change the way he looked at her by planting the idea in his head that she considered herself to be too heavy.

Right now, when Dillon looked at her, she didn't feel fat, anyway. She felt desirable.

And maybe because he'd known her before she'd become famous, she felt as if his wanting her mattered somehow, as if he truly wanted Ashley Wilde, not the cover girl.

Recognizing the unique power he held over her, she realized that that made her vulnerable to him. And with his promise to seduce her lingering in the air between them, every moment they spent together spelled danger.

Oddly enough, though, with the night air cool and whisper soft with just a hint of rain, she found she didn't care so much about the danger. In fact, she was beginning to wonder if being here with Dillon wasn't the first risk she'd faced worth taking in a very long time.

Long after Ashley had gone off to bed, Dillon lingered on the deck. The temperature had indeed dropped after sunset, but he didn't mind the sharp bite to the air. He zipped up his leather jacket, propped his feet on the railing and stared into the clear night sky, trying to recall the last time he'd ever felt so much at peace.

The truth of it was, though, he couldn't think of a single moment. The day he'd opened his security agency came close. Seeing his name on the door of that first tiny office had brought him an astonishing sense of satisfaction. Signing his first big client later that same day had proved that Trent Wilde's faith in him hadn't been misplaced.

He wondered what Ashley would think if she knew just exactly how big a role her father had played in his life. It was Trent who'd bailed him out of the Riverton jail years ago. And it was Trent who'd had a quiet word with the judge and seen to it that the flimsy case against him for a robbery he hadn't committed was dropped.

There wasn't a doubt in Dillon's mind that without Trent's intervention, he would have served serious jail time despite the lack of hard evidence against him. Too many people in Riverton were quick to jump to conclusions about him and eager to blame him for crimes they didn't want to know had been committed by their own children.

He'd never known exactly why Trent had leapt to his defense, but he'd sworn never to let him down after that. And when his mentor had advised him to leave Riverton for a while and make something of himself where his past wouldn't be thrown in his face, Dillon had climbed onto his Harley and taken off. His only regret back then was that he would never know what might have been between him and Ashley Wilde.

This accidental encounter would give him a chance to discover if his adolescent crush truly meant anything. He wondered what Trent would do if he knew Dillon was locked away up here with his youngest daughter. When asking about Trent's family, Dillon had always tried very hard never to mention Ashley any more than Sara or Dani. If his eagerness for news of Ashley had been evident, Trent had never let on.

Despite the closeness he and Trent shared, Dillon had always feared there might be unspoken limits. He'd figured a relationship between him and Ashley might top the list.

But though he never wanted to betray the older man's trust in him, Dillon had recognized in the past twenty-four hours that nothing would stand between him and Ashley this time. There was a fragility to her now that intrigued and worried him. Something or someone had hurt her, and he aimed to find out how. If it was within his power, he would fix things for her.

He figured he owed it to himself, too, to find out if, as he'd always suspected, she really was the only woman in the world for him. Or if he'd just built up a world-class fantasy about the one girl he'd never had. He could only pray that Trent would never put his loyalty to the test by asking Dillon to walk away from his daughter.

Despite his late-night wrestling with his conscience, Dillon was up at the crack of dawn the next morning. Even so, Ashley was up ahead of him. He found her at the kitchen table with a half a grapefruit in front of her and a sour expression on her face. He suspected that expression had less to do with the taste of her meal than with its sparseness.

"How about some scrambled eggs?" he asked cheerfully and earned a scowl and a curt refusal.

"Toast, then?"

"No, thank you."

"If you don't eat, then I can't take you with me

today,'' he said as he whisked three eggs and dumped them into a skillet sizzling with butter.

''Oh?'' she said, looking ever-so-slightly intrigued.

''I was thinking of a picnic.''

She sighed. ''More food.''

''After a long hike,'' he amended. ''A very long hike.''

''I suppose that could be fun,'' she admitted grudgingly.

''It's another gorgeous day,'' he said. ''The rain stopped before dawn.''

''You were awake that early?''

''Just taking advantage of opportunity,'' he taunted. ''But I'm not taking you, if you're going to pass out halfway there from lack of food.''

She rolled her eyes, but she accepted the plate of scrambled eggs he held out. And the toast. She did ignore the butter, which he placed prominently in front of her, and the orange marmalade. He chose to let that pass.

He ate his breakfast, then sat back and studied her over the rim of his coffee mug. Eventually she lifted her gaze from her plate and stared at him defiantly.

''Is there something on your mind?'' she asked.

''I was just wondering what all those admiring hordes would think if they could see you now.''

Immediately, she touched a self-conscious hand to her casually caught-up hairstyle. ''I'm a mess,'' she said. ''Don't remind me.''

''You are not a mess,'' he contradicted. ''You

look more natural and more beautiful than you ever have on any magazine cover.''

She stared at him, mouth gaping. ''You're crazy.''

''Nope. I don't think so. You have color in your cheeks that doesn't come from any cosmetic I've ever seen.''

''Because you're making me blush.''

''Whatever. And your lips look extraordinarily kissable,'' he added, enjoying the way that deepened the pink tone in her cheeks. ''As for your hair, no man could resist the urge to tug away that silly ribbon or whatever it is that's holding it up.''

To prove it, he stood and reached behind her to release waves of blond silk. The wayward curls tumbled past her shoulders. Ashley tried to scoop them back into the careless ponytail, but Dillon prevented it with a touch.

''Don't. It's magnificent.''

''It hasn't been properly styled in days. My stylist would have a heart attack if he saw it.''

He grinned at the complaint. ''There are millions of women in the world who'd like their hair to be half so incredible after a few days in the middle of nowhere.''

Her gaze locked with his, and he thought he read complete bafflement in her eyes. That hint of uncertainty startled him. How could Ashley Wilde, admired by millions, be uncertain about anything?

''How do you do that?'' she asked.

''What?''

''The impossible. I woke up this morning feeling

miserable and dowdy, and with no more than a few glib words, you've turned that around."

"Sweetheart, you couldn't look dowdy decked out in your grandmother's worst muslin frock."

She grinned. "Frock? Dillon, where do you spend your time?"

"I read one of my sister's historical romances once," he said, then added quickly, "purely as research, of course. I wanted to be able to carry on a conversation about something that actually mattered to her. At any rate, the heroine was very big on frocks. She had a wardrobe filled with them, as I recall."

Ashley's eyes danced with amusement. "And did this research pay off? Did you and your sister have a meaningful conversation as a result?"

"Actually, no. I was too afraid she'd want to talk about the love scenes, and that was definitely not a conversation I intended to have with her."

"Somehow I can't imagine you ever being unwilling to discuss sex," she said.

"Not with my sister. She was a baby at the time."

"How old?" she asked, laughing, no doubt at his horrified expression.

"Sixteen," he admitted. "But that was too young for sex."

"Maybe to do it, but obviously not to read about it," Ashley said. "Somebody should have discussed it with her."

"I asked one of my girlfriends to do it. She knew more about sex than any book I ever read."

"Oh, really?"

She looked so thoroughly indignant that Dillon chuckled. "Jealous, sweetheart?"

"Hardly."

"It was ten years ago, you know."

"Whatever you did ten years ago or two days ago is none of my business," she said stiffly.

"Exactly."

She peered at him. "But what have you been doing all these years?"

"So much for leaving the past in the past," he noted. "But I'll indulge you on this one point. No marriages. No serious long-term relationships."

"Ah, commitment phobic, then," she said knowingly.

He stared straight into her eyes and waited a beat before declaring softly, "No, just committed to finding the right person before I jump into anything that's supposed to last till death do us part."

He watched as she swallowed hard and tried to tear her gaze away from his face.

"I think maybe we'd better go for that walk," she said in a voice that sounded slightly breathless.

"Afraid of what'll happen if we stay here?"

Her chin tilted defiantly. "I am not the least bit afraid of you, Dillon Ford. But I just ate more calories and cholesterol than any human being should consume at daybreak. It's time to work it off."

"Have I mentioned that this obsession you have with the fat content of food is a little twisted?" Dillon asked.

"If you read the newspapers or watched TV news, you'd know it's not possible to be too obsessed with what we eat. Everyone should be concerned about it, not just models."

"If you declare that we are what we eat, I may have to stuff a rag in your mouth," he warned.

Apparently he'd managed exactly the dead-serious tone he'd intended, because she was regarding him warily. "You wouldn't dare," she said.

"Try me," he said grimly. "And before you ask, I'm packing our picnic and you'll eat what I bring, are we clear?"

"Do you have control issues?" she inquired testily.

"If you're asking if I tend to take charge, then the answer is yes. I find it saves a lot of time."

"Ever hear of compromise?"

"Sweetheart, when you offer a compromise worth considering, I'll compromise."

"How gallant!"

"I do try. Now scoot, so I can get this picnic packed."

"Afraid I'll try to sneak in some carrot sticks?"

"No, I just work faster alone."

"No wonder you've never married," she observed dryly.

Dillon grinned. "Sweetheart, you've just hit on the one area where I do believe that two is better than one. We could abandon this hike and I could demonstrate, if you like."

"Marriage isn't only about sex," she reminded him.

"Maybe not," he agreed readily. "But without it, things would definitely be a whole lot duller."

Apparently Ashley had no argument for that, because she backed out of the kitchen and retreated to the front porch. That was where he found her when he finished preparing their picnic. She glanced up as he came through the door, two backpacks in hand. She held out her hand for hers, then hefted it gingerly.

"There's definitely not an entire roast in here, so I suppose I should be grateful."

"How do you know it's not in mine?" he taunted.

"Care to trade with me?"

"No way," he said. "You're clearly a woman who's been deprived of chocolate for far too long. I'm not putting these candy bars into your safekeeping."

She promptly ran her tongue over her lips in an unconscious gesture that had Dillon's blood pumping like an oil well.

"Ah," he said. "I see I've struck a nerve."

"You have chocolate in there?" she asked, her gaze pinned on his backpack.

"Several bars," he confirmed, enjoying the pure greed suddenly shining in her eyes.

"That is a very dangerous admission," she warned him.

"Oh? You thinking of trying to get them away from me?"

"I'm thinking of killing you for them."

Dillon's hoot of laughter carried on the clear morning air. "Sweetheart, I always dreamed of leading you astray. I just never dreamed all it would take was a candy bar."

Chapter Five

Ashley had never wanted so badly to be led astray in her entire, orderly life.

Forget the chocolate...although she was having a difficult time doing that. It was Dillon who truly tempted her. In fact, he was driving her crazy with his compliments and his seductive looks and his provocative conversation.

She desperately needed what he was offering. She needed to feel desirable, and he accomplished that in spades. In fact, if she didn't start expending some energy on that promised hike in the next few seconds, she was very likely to tackle him where he stood. Maybe it wouldn't solve all her self-esteem problems, but it would go a long way toward making her forget them for a short while. Surely she wouldn't be the first woman to use Dillon as a sex object. She doubted he'd mind at all.

Maybe her on-the-edge hunger was in her eyes or in her tone, because he suddenly set off toward the woods at a brisk, punishing pace. No wonder he'd said a big breakfast was no problem. At the rate he moved, they'd work off the calories in the first half-hour.

Even with her comfortably long strides, she had difficulty keeping up with him. Since the path he chose was straight uphill and she refused to plead for mercy, she was breathless by the time he finally paused for a rest. She quickly accepted the bottled water he offered and drank thirstily.

"Have you ever considered becoming a personal trainer?" she asked. "You set a brutal pace."

He instantly looked contrite. "Why didn't you say something? I would have slowed down."

For some reason, the comment rankled. "I didn't say I couldn't keep up," she retorted.

"Of course not," he said.

He said it in such a placating, patronizing tone that Ashley had to grit her teeth to keep from cursing. That was exactly the kind of attitude that could rid her of any romantic fantasies about this man.

She sighed at the direction her thoughts had taken only a short time before. What had ever made her think she could put up with a chauvinistic, testosterone-laden male for more than a few hours at a time? Her father was evidence enough that such men were impossible. Dillon, for reasons she had yet to understand, seemed to be one of Trent Wilde's disciples. Some lessons, at least, he'd learned very well.

Or was he one of those lost causes her father periodically took under his wing? Once again she began to wonder just what had brought this unlikely pair together. And exactly what had Dillon been doing with his life since he scooted out of Riverton in the dark of night years earlier?

Her initial assumption that he was in some kind of desperate trouble was beginning to seem less and less likely. He hadn't seemed the least bit concerned that they'd been seen at the store. In fact, he'd been less worried about it than she had, which must prove something about him being innocent of any crime.

Whatever he had been doing, though, it must have included rigorous fitness training, she concluded as Dillon practically sprinted off uphill again. Thankful for all those tedious step-aerobics and weight-training classes, she trailed after him, albeit at a more leisurely pace.

"Do you have any idea where you're going?" she called out eventually as the woods grew denser and she could no longer hear the babbling of the stream that edged her father's property.

He glanced over his shoulder and grinned. "If where we're going really matters to you, isn't that something you should have asked an hour ago?"

"Probably," she conceded, then persisted, "do you know?"

"Always," he said. "You're not scared just because there are no street signs and stoplights, are you?"

"I have to admit, I'd feel better if there was at least some sign of a trail underfoot."

He winked. "There is. You just have to have a trained eye to spot it."

Ashley regarded him skeptically. That didn't sound at all like the boy she'd known, who'd always struck her as someone who'd be more at home in an urban jungle than some dark tangle of weeds, trees and underbrush. She'd always assumed she knew exactly how he spent his spare time back then, but maybe there were aspects of his past not even she knew.

"Did you get some sort of wilderness training I don't know about?"

"Surely you're not asking if I was ever a Boy Scout?" he replied, looking as appalled as if she'd suggested he'd secretly taken home economics.

Ashley chuckled. "No, believe me, that thought never once crossed my mind. They would probably have thrown you out by the time you turned twelve."

"I was ten, actually."

He said it with a contradictory mix of pride and chagrin. The glint in his eyes suggested pride was winning. He always had seemed to relish his reputation as a bad boy.

"Did you enjoy turning the troop upside down?" she asked.

"Immensely," he admitted with a grin. "My father was appalled. He thought the troop would straighten me out, give me a sense of direction, teach me some values. Unfortunately, they never gave patches for the sort of things I was interested in."

"Such as?"

"I'm sure you can imagine."

"You were interested in girls at the age of ten?" she asked incredulously.

"I think maybe I'll plead the Fifth on that one." He eyed her curiously. "So, what were you really asking a minute ago when you mentioned wilderness training?"

"I just thought perhaps you'd been through the Trent Wilde school of wilderness adventures."

"Uh-oh," he said, looking fascinated. "You don't say that fondly."

"Actually, I missed the worst of it. Daddy wanted sons. He expected sons. Three girls were a surprise, but he remained undaunted," she said. "He put Dani through his own brand of survival training in the wilds. She hasn't set foot in the cabin since. She won't even build a fire in her fireplace. And she absolutely shudders at the mention of rabbit stew and venison steak."

Dillon laughed. "I'm surprised Trent hasn't disowned her."

"Believe me, the thought probably crossed his mind a time or two. On the other hand," Ashley continued. "Sara loved it so much she ran off and spent days on end hiding out somewhere up here when Daddy threatened to send her off to finishing school. She turned everything he'd taught her against him."

Dillon's grin broadened. "He told me about that."

"He told everyone about it," Ashley said dryly. "It was hard to tell if he was furious or pleased, but after that, he pretty much gave up. I guess he figured he was no match for our individual preferences and stubbornness, or else he just accepted the fact that girls would never love the same things that sons might have."

"He let you off the hook? That doesn't sound like him."

"Actually, by the time he dragged me up here, he just handed me a fishing pole and pointed me in the direction of the stream. He didn't even complain when I tossed back everything I caught."

"Oh, but what a disappointment you must have been to him," Dillon teased.

"It was no laughing matter, I'll have you know. But that was the least of the ways I disappointed him, actually," she said with an air of resignation. "My determination to move to New York was the real biggie."

Dillon's expression sobered at once. "No, it wasn't," he said adamantly. He regarded her curiously. "Don't you know how proud he is of you? My God, Ashley, he has drawers filled with every magazine you've ever appeared in. He has framed pictures on the wall in his office."

"You've been to Three-Stars?" For some reason that startled her even more than his familiarity with the cabin or his apparent understanding of her father's thoughts about the life she'd chosen.

The cabin was her father's private sanctuary, but Three-Stars was as public as a governor's mansion, a place where Trent showed off his wealth and power. That Dillon had been invited there showed a level of acceptance, a certain depth of male bonding and respect between the two men that she hadn't guessed existed, despite Dillon's claims that the two were friends.

"It's not Buckingham Palace, sweetheart. It doesn't require an invitation from the Queen."

Naturally, she thought, Dillon had managed to totally misunderstand and find an insult where none had been intended. "You know what I mean," she said.

"No, I don't. Your father's not the snob you seem to think he is. Or is it just that you can't imagine anyone inviting me into their home?"

Ashley could feel a dull red flush creeping up her neck. "That isn't what I meant at all. It's just that I'm still struggling with the idea that you and my father are friends. He's so..."

"Respectable," Dillon offered.

She didn't like the stiff, cool way he said it, but she nodded. "Okay, yes. Trent Wilde is the epitome of respectability."

A warning spark flashed in Dillon's eyes. "And I am...?"

Ashley wouldn't have answered that if all the hounds of hell had been nipping at her heels. Dillon's expression demanded a diplomatic answer, and she couldn't think of anything remotely tactful. Respectability had never been a word she would have applied to the Dillon of old.

"Trouble?" he suggested, filling in the blank for her. "A grown-up version of a juvenile delinquent? Have I hit it yet or should I keep going?"

Ashley swallowed hard at the sudden anger blazing in his eyes. "The truth is I don't know you at all," she admitted softly.

"That's right, you don't. So maybe you should reserve judgment on whether or not your father's a fool for befriending me."

His anger was palpable and, she felt, unjustified. "I never said that," she said indignantly.

"Maybe not in those precise words, but the message was clear enough."

"Or maybe you just have a giant-size chip on your shoulder."

"If I do, people like you put it there." With that he whipped off his backpack and dropped it on the ground at her feet. "Enjoy your picnic, sweetheart. Suddenly I'm not very hungry."

He was gone before Ashley could gather her wits to chase after him. Mouth open, she watched as he vanished into the woods. She had two choices. She could try to catch up to him and apologize or she could retreat and make her way to the cabin, where he was bound to turn up eventually.

She decided on the latter. Maybe it was cowardice or maybe it was just the certain knowledge that Dillon needed time to cool down before he would hear any apology she offered. Obviously, she had inadvertently touched a raw nerve. Perhaps, for all the enjoyment he seemed to take in bucking the establishment, he didn't like being labeled an outcast, after all.

And the truth was, just as she had admitted to him, she had no idea what kind of man he'd become. All she really knew was that she was deeply attracted to him, no matter what grievous sins he might have committed.

Dillon couldn't imagine what had gotten into him back there. Surely after all these years he should have developed a thick skin when it came to disparaging looks or unwarranted comments. Growing up in Riverton, where judgments were quick and lasting, had been good training. And in fact, only a couple of days before he'd exalted at being thought of once again as a rebel, a bad boy or whatever particular label had stuck in Ashley's head.

Maybe it wasn't the label so much that bothered him. Maybe it was some subtle difference he'd detected in her attitude.

From the moment of his arrival, there'd been no mistaking the sexual tension blazing between the two of them. She wanted him just as badly as he wanted her.

But just now, as they'd hiked through the woods, she'd hinted that while he might be good enough to sleep with, exciting enough for a quick roll in the sack, he might not be decent enough to be friends with the lofty likes of Trent Wilde.

Ironically, of course, that was far from Trent's view. And, even more ironically, it hurt worse coming from Ashley, a woman who by her own admission didn't really know him at all.

The fact that it was based on a misapprehension on her part didn't seem to matter. She'd judged him and found him wanting based on absolutely nothing but the past, and half of that she only knew because she'd heard it repeated a thousand times.

That told him quite a lot about the woman she was. He'd joked before about her being a snob, but he'd just discovered it was no laughing matter when he was on the receiving end of her unspoken disdain.

Of course, none of that kept him from wanting her. His hunger for her nagged at him like a persistent mosquito and, under the circumstances, was a hundred times more infuriating. How could he want a woman who thought so little of him?

All the way to the cabin, Dillon told himself he ought to cut his losses and find some other place to hide out for the remainder of his self-imposed exile from the L.A. rat race. But he knew he wouldn't. He had something to prove, to himself, if not to Ashley.

He was going to win her over and he was going to do it on his own terms, without revealing that he was no longer an outsider, but a part of the establishment. Maybe in the process he'd discover why all the success he'd achieved didn't matter nearly as much as he'd once expected it to.

Or maybe the real truth was that all the respect in the world couldn't make up for his inability to impress the one woman who'd ever really mattered to him.

She was gone! Dillon called out to Ashley from the front porch, then again from the living room. She didn't answer. A search of the cabin turned up no sign of her.

Acid churned in the pit of his stomach. What if she'd simply taken off? What if he never saw her again?

Well, that wouldn't happen, he vowed. He was no longer an adolescent, forced to leave home in order to have any hope of a future. He had almost unlimited financial resources and a large staff of very savvy private eyes working for him. He could find her even if she never again appeared on the cover of a magazine, even if she took to hiding out in the most remote corner of the earth.

And of course, he had a single ace up his sleeve—her father. Wherever Ashley disappeared to, sooner or later she'd be in touch with Trent. Dillon was confident he could persuade his friend to share that information.

And he would do just that, he promised himself. It wasn't over between him and Ashley. Not by a long shot.

Just as he was working himself into a genuine frenzy of anticipation over the impending search for the elusive Ashley Wilde, the woman herself turned into the driveway at a speed more suited to a raceway. Gravel flew as she screeched to a halt. Dillon stood on the front porch and watched her approach with a wild mix of relief and irritation that her return mattered so damned much. A few hours earlier he'd been furious with her, insulted by her, and now he was practically jubilant at her return.

It would never do, though, to let her see that he'd been worried for a minute by her absence. He forced himself into a chair, propped his feet on the railing and leaned back as if he couldn't possibly be any more relaxed or unconcerned. He regretted with all his heart that he didn't have a beer to sip or a cigarette to smoke.

Fortunately, his sunglasses kept her from spotting the avid way he observed her exit from the car, one exquisite, bare leg after the other. Those shorts she wore ought to be outlawed, he thought, swallowing hard as they inched up her thigh.

As she crossed to the porch, she smiled tentatively. "Cooled off yet?"

Not by a long shot, Dillon thought, though he doubted they meant the same thing. "Some," he said.

"I'm sorry if I offended you earlier. I didn't mean to."

"People never do," he observed coolly.

Temper flared in her eyes. "I'm not *people,*" she retorted. "And if you can't accept a sincere apology when it's offered, then you're the one with the real problem."

"Could be," he conceded.

That seemed to stop whatever she'd been about to say next. She stared at him warily.

"You're admitting what happened up there was your fault as much as mine?" she asked.

He shrugged. "More or less."

Her lips twitched ever so slightly. "Am I to assume that's as close to an apology as I'm likely to get?"

"You can assume whatever you like, sweetheart. You usually do."

"Dillon, that is not the way to go about making peace," she chided. "You're starting the war all over again."

"So sorry. I surrender."

She shook her head. "I doubt that."

Dillon decided to move on to what he really wanted to know. "Where have you been, anyway?" He actually managed to sound only casually interested, he thought with satisfaction. An observer—or more important, Ashley herself—would never guess how much the answer mattered.

"Did you miss me?" she asked.

Okay, so she was onto him. He didn't have to admit to anything.

"Like a toothache," he said. "Who wouldn't miss this scintillating war of words? I asked a simple question. If you don't want to answer, just say so."

"I went for a drive. You stalk off in a huff when you're angry. I drive."

He found the revelation illuminating. "In that case, it must have been frustrating living in New York all those years. Or did jumping into a taxi work just as well?"

"Very funny."

"No, seriously, what did you do to relieve stress? As competitive as modeling is, there had to have been a lot of tension."

"Enough," she said succinctly. "I meditated."

"Did it work?"

"Not nearly as well as sparring for an hour with a punching bag."

Dillon chuckled despite himself. "You boxed?"

Her expression turned sheepish. "Well, I never got into a ring, exactly, but yes. I put a mental image of whoever was driving me nuts onto that bag and slugged away. It was very satisfying. I mentally bloodied the noses of a lot of very important people in the business."

"I'll bet. I suppose my face would have been on there this afternoon."

"Right in the middle of the mental bull's-eye," she agreed cheerfully. "But I'm over that now."

"Must have been some drive."

She looked straight into his eyes. "Must have been some hike."

"Touché."

She settled her tush onto the railing right next to his propped-up feet. "Now that we've made peace, let's start fresh. Let's pretend we've just met for the first time. Why don't you tell me who Dillon Ford is today? All of the relevant statistics—where you live, what you do, who you date."

That would be the easy way, but Dillon had never opted for easy in his life. He shook his head. "I don't think so. I think maybe that's one you should figure out for yourself."

She regarded him worriedly. "Why? Is there something you're trying to hide?"

There was no mistaking her meaning or the tiny flicker of unease in her eyes. Dillon gave her a hard stare and asked, "You mean am I wanted for any major crimes?"

She winced at that. Before she could try to wriggle off that particular hook, Dillon took pity on her. As insulting as he found the question, he supposed she had a right to ask, was even smart to ask, for that matter. After all, she was all alone with him here. And though she obviously didn't feel herself to be in any danger—except perhaps from her hormones—some level of concern was clearly nagging at her.

"No, sweetheart. I will tell you that much. My slate is clean with the law. There won't be any cops arriving at the front door to interrupt us."

He watched closely for her reaction to his declaration. She didn't look either relieved or disappointed. She simply nodded, accepting what he said as truth, apparently.

"I'll go fix dinner," she told him, and headed for the door.

"Ashley?" Dillon called after her.

"What?"

"I'm very sorry you felt you had to ask."

She sighed. "Me, too."

Chapter Six

Ashley had no idea what to make of Dillon's odd mood or her own. As relieved as she'd been by his response to her pointed question about whether he was hiding out, she also felt an amazing amount of guilt over having raised the issue at all.

It had been an insulting question. If she'd been on the receiving end of it, she doubted she would still be sharing a house with the person who'd asked.

The possibility that he might yet decide to walk out on her terrified her. She found that she didn't want to be alone. More, she didn't want to lose this chance to discover if she and Dillon had anything more in common than mutual lust and old yearnings.

And yet she wouldn't blame him if he left.

Not that Dillon seemed to be holding her question against her. He'd chatted pleasantly all through dinner, though there was an unmistakable distance between them that had never been there before, not even years ago.

She couldn't blame him for that, either. She should have trusted her gut feeling that deep down Dillon was honest, kind and caring. Since his unexpected arrival here, when he'd discovered her already occupying the space he'd expected to find empty, he'd been all of those things, in spite of her lack of welcome. Her only excuse for prodding was that she didn't trust her own judgment about much of anything these days, least of all men.

It didn't help that Dillon intentionally diverted attention away from himself and focused on her. She supposed she ought to be flattered, but she was so used to men whose monumental egos required they be the center of attention that Dillon's actions seemed suspect.

Add to that her current low level of self-esteem, which left her convinced no one as sexy as Dillon could possibly be interested in her unless he had an ulterior motive, and she was left struggling with all sorts of doubts and dire warnings.

She finished washing the dishes and stared into the living room where Dillon had gone right after dinner. Despite his all-black attire and too-long hair, he looked perfectly at home. He looked like a man who knew who he was and was thoroughly comfortable with himself and his environment. She found that almost as disconcerting as the way he so easily provoked a sensual response from her body.

He was sitting in one of her father's overstuffed

leather chairs reading some book he'd plucked from the shelves. Given the dull topics of most of those books, she couldn't imagine what he found so fascinating. As far as she knew, he had no particular interest in either fishing or cattle, but it was evident he was totally absorbed.

As far as she knew... Of course, that was the real crux of the problem. She didn't know a darn thing, and he didn't seem inclined to change that.

I think I'll let you figure that out for yourself. What the devil was that supposed to mean? she wondered irritably.

Suddenly she recalled her own words the night before. She'd been complaining about men never looking beyond her glamorous image, about them never seeing her. Wasn't that really what Dillon was asking of her? Didn't he simply want her to get to know him for who he was and not be distracted by her memory of the way he had once been or by whatever it was he did for a living? Good or bad.

She felt like charging into the living room and announcing, "I get it."

Well, she concluded, there was more than one way to pry information out of someone who'd clammed up. She'd tried the direct approach. Obviously, it was time to use more subtle techniques. She would do as he preferred and gather clues from his behavior and from dropped hints about his life. She simply had to create an environment in which hints were likely to be dropped.

There was no time like the present to start. Studying Dillon promised to be far more intriguing than wrestling with her own problems. He promised to be an incredible diversion. She began by walking into the living room and asking if he wanted to play cards or a game.

"I think there's a Monopoly set here somewhere," she added.

She'd discovered in New York and on the road that a rowdy round of Monopoly or any other game often told her a lot about a person's need to win, his quick-wittedness and his greed. Men who refused to play any game at all were generally too stuffy to bear. She waited anxiously to see which category Dillon fell into.

"How about chess?" he asked, readily putting aside the book. "Your father and I get the board out first thing when we're here. He told me that you, Sara and Dani all play."

Ashley grinned. "Who wins when you play Daddy?"

"I do. Why?"

"I just like to know ahead of time if I'm likely to get trounced."

"Are you a sore loser?"

"Sometimes."

The somber expression he'd worn all evening gave way to a grin. "Me, too."

"Then it should be an interesting evening, shouldn't it?"

He shot her a wry look. "With you and me in the same room, sweetheart, it couldn't be anything else," he said in a way that sent goose bumps chasing down her spine.

"You get the board," she said in a breathless rush. "I'll get us something to drink. What would you like? Coffee? Beer? Whiskey?"

"I'm tempted to finish off that bottle of twelve-year-old special-blend Scotch your father brought back from Glasgow and has hidden away, but I think I'll stick to beer."

"Afraid he'd check for fingerprints on the bottle?"

"No, sweetheart. I want to keep all my wits about me for the game." He shot a knowing look at her. "And after."

Ashley felt her throat close up. Apparently he wasn't holding a grudge. She practically ran from the room. In the kitchen, she filled a glass with water and drank every cooling drop. She barely resisted the urge to splash some on her overheated face.

When she'd salvaged her composure, she returned to the living room with Dillon's bottle of beer and her coffee. If he thought he needed his wits about him, she wanted a large dose of caffeine to bolster her own.

Dillon had set up the old board that had belonged to her grandfather. As a child, before this chess set had been moved from Three-Stars to the cabin, she had loved to touch the smooth ivory pieces. When her father had finally agreed to teach her the game, she had felt so grown-up.

"Why the smile?" Dillon asked.

"I was just remembering the first time Daddy played chess with me. I felt as if it were some sort of rite of passage."

"How old were you?"

"Eight, maybe. Until then I had been so envious of Dani and Sara. Daddy played chess with them practically every evening after dinner. First one and then the other. It never took him long to beat them."

"I suppose you vowed then and there that you'd be the first one to beat him."

"Of course."

"Did you?"

"Just once." She chuckled at the memory of her father's expression when she'd suggested the stakes. "We bet my future. If I won, I got to go to New York and he'd stake me for the first year. If I lost, I promised to go off to some suitable college and get some disgustingly practical degree the same way Sara and Dani had."

Dillon whistled. "You must have been awfully confident."

She shook her head. "No, desperate, really. I knew if I didn't do something totally outrageous, he'd never believe I was serious about going. He'd bully me until I wound up with a degree in accounting or computer science so I could keep the ranch's books for him."

Dillon shook his head. "You and your sister must be big on outrageous bets."

At her quizzical look, he explained, "I heard about Sara betting Jake that she could beat him in bronc riding to win the ranch. Obviously neither of you would flinch at the role of the dice in Vegas, no matter how much you had on the table."

Ashley grinned. "If the stakes aren't big enough,

what's the point? Besides, don't let Jake kid you. He was betting as much for Sara as he was for the ranch."

"Remind me not to gamble on anything major with any of you. So, how long did it take you to win the chess match with your father?"

"Two days," she recalled. "We played until after midnight, until Mother insisted we go to bed because I had school in the morning. We finished the next night. He had me checked three or four times, scared the daylights out of me, but I managed to wriggle out and stay in the game. When I finally said checkmate, I'm not sure which of us was more stunned."

"What did he say? Do you remember?"

"Sure. He asked me if I wanted to make it the best two out of three," she said, laughing. "He never gave up."

"But he gave you your stake and let you go without any more arguments, didn't he?"

"Without more arguments? You must be kidding. But, yes, he let me go and he financed that first year. He grumbled all the time, though."

"Just to keep you on your toes," Dillon assured her. "He always told me that getting you set up in New York was the best investment he ever made because it had made you happy. He told me that a man's greatest accomplishment was the happiness of his children. If he achieved that, then he'd done okay."

Holding a pawn in his hand to make his first move, Dillon fixed his gaze on her. "Moving to

New York, becoming a model has made you happy, hasn't it?''

Ashley shrugged and evaded that penetrating stare. ''Every job has its ups and downs, but on the whole, yes. I've been happy.''

''How come you can't look me straight in the eyes when you say that?'' he asked.

She forced her gaze to meet his. ''Do I need to say it again to make *you* happy?''

He studied her intently for the space of a heartbeat, then shook his head. ''No, I'll accept your earlier statement for now.'' He reached across the table and tucked a finger under her chin. ''But sooner or later, we'll get into whatever's troubling you, sweetheart. Count on it.''

''Why does it matter to you whether or not I'm content with my career? A few more days, a week and you'll be gone. I'll be the last thing on your mind.''

''Don't sell yourself short, angel. It would take more than a little time and distance for a man to forget you.''

He sounded so thoroughly, beguilingly sincere that Ashley's heart began to thump unsteadily. She slowly lifted her gaze and searched his face, looking for some clue that would prove what was really in his heart. His eyes blazed with blatant lust as he deliberately, provocatively locked gazes with her. Her pulse ricocheted wildly.

''Do you really want to play chess?'' he asked quietly.

The words barely registered. ''Hmm?''

"Are you going to be able to keep your mind on the game?"

"What game?"

His lips curved in a lazy, satisfied smile. "Precisely my point."

Because she wasn't crazy about the implication that he could distract her so easily, Ashley forced her attention to the chessboard. The prospect of playing had never struck her as duller, especially with that promising gleam in Dillon's eyes as competition. Why not just have the fling she so obviously craved and be done with it? It was way past time for her to flirt a bit with danger.

She looked up until their gazes caught again, then she slowly, deliberately swept her hand across the board, tumbling the chess pieces from their places.

"I guess the game's over," Dillon observed.

"I don't know," Ashley said softly. "It seems to me as if it's just begun."

The taunt was very effective. Dillon stood in such a rush that the small table between them wobbled dangerously. He cast it aside as if it was no more than a troublesome fleck of dust, then reached for her.

All her doubts about him fled in that instant, lost to a more pressing hunger. Ashley moved into his arms with the inevitability of metal being drawn by a powerful magnet. His mouth settled on hers in a coaxing kiss that stole breath and thought.

While that first memorable kiss they'd shared a few days before had been greedy and demanding, this kiss was all about persuasion. Sweet and gentle and warm as a summer shower, the kiss teased and taunted until Ashley melted in Dillon's arms. He could have lured her anywhere with the seductiveness of his lips on hers.

Instead, though, he seemed content to explore all the possible nuances of kissing. In time, sweet and gentle escalated to dark and mysterious and from there to a passion so all-consuming, so hot that Ashley wondered how she'd ever imagined any other kiss to be anything more than adequate.

By the time his tongue dipped into her mouth, she was lost. As the swirling heat low in her belly grew more and more demanding, she knew that whatever kind of man Dillon had become, he was quite possibly the only man on earth who could stir the promise of such pleasure.

His hands slid over her body in light strokes that left behind fire. He tucked her hips more tightly against the cradle of his thighs. Heat flared, so much heat that Ashley thought she would be consumed by it.

And then something changed. She heard him sigh, felt his hands still where they rested on her hips. When he pulled away, she felt bereft.

"Dillon," she pleaded, leaving the rest unspoken. He knew what she wanted, what she so desperately needed. She could read the understanding of it in his hooded gaze, in the smug curve of his lips.

But even though it was painfully obvious that he wanted the same thing, that his body was as aroused as hers, he merely touched a finger to her lips, skimming the curve in a gesture that made her blood run hot all over again. She could feel the wild tingling all the way to her toes.

"Dillon," she cried out again, her voice little more than a ragged whisper.

"Slow down, sweetheart," he said, his voice raw with an unmistakable primal need.

"Why?"

The question drew a grin. "Because you'd hate me in the morning."

"I wouldn't," Ashley swore vehemently.

"Sure you would. Or, if not me, then yourself. When you and I make love...and we will," he assured her, "it will be because you want me, the real me, not who you think I am. It won't just be a rebellion."

His analysis of her motivations was as effective as being dashed with ice water.

"I'm not rebelling," she insisted, despite her own nagging doubts that that was precisely what she was doing. "And if you think that's what this is about then you don't know *me,* either."

"Oh, but I do," he said smugly. "I always have, even way back in high school when you were tempted so badly you ached with it."

The arrogant assumption that she'd been panting after him even then infuriated her. Unfortunately, it hit too close to the truth for her to be able to deny it with any sort of conviction, so she kept her mouth clamped tightly shut.

Instead, she gathered her pride and forced herself to brush a nonchalant kiss across his cheek.

"Too bad you picked tonight to develop a conscience, Dillon. You don't know what you've missed."

"Oh, it's not over between us, Ashley. You can count on that."

She trembled at the promise in his voice, but she managed to escape to her bedroom before he could see the tears of humiliation and pure frustration that were brimming in her eyes.

For all Dillon's taunts and innuendos about the future, she was convinced she knew the real reason he'd stopped his seduction tonight. At some point he'd realized that she was no longer the perfect size six, glamorous beauty who'd once taken the modeling world by storm. The attraction he'd once felt for her had died.

It didn't really matter that all the evidence pointed to the contrary. It didn't matter that she knew with absolute certainty he was every bit as aroused as she was. This didn't have anything to do with reason or logic or common sense. It had everything to do with self-esteem that was in the toilet and one trusted man's assurances that she'd lost her glamour and seductiveness.

Now she had her proof. She'd failed to seduce the only man she'd ever really wanted, and his rejection hurt. It didn't seem to matter that his motives sounded noble and honest and sincere. It only mattered that Dillon had inadvertently reinforced every negative perception she had of herself.

She'd thought that brutal meeting with her agent had been the low point of her life, but she'd been mistaken. Tonight had been personal and far more devastating.

Dillon couldn't believe he had just let Ashley walk out of his arms and out of the room to sleep alone. As she'd said, it was a damnable time to develop a conscience.

But despite their growing rapport, despite their constant physical awareness, he couldn't ignore the fact that on some deep level Ashley was struggling with herself about whether she could trust him.

She was also struggling with other demons that he had yet to put a finger on. For the past few days he'd seen hurt and confusion and doubt in her eyes, and he knew those things had nothing to do with him. Sometimes she looked so lost and shattered he ached to take her into his arms and reassure her. But that would inevitably lead to lovemaking, and until he understood what was going on in her head, how could he risk adding to her pain?

Was she here to recover from a love affair gone sour? The very idea of her caring that much about another man made his stomach churn. He wanted to believe she had never been as sweetly sensual or as wildly passionate with anyone as she had been in his arms only moments before. He wanted to believe the unmistakable link between them was as rare and unexpected for her as it was for him.

Not that his motive in pushing her away tonight had been totally altruistic, he admitted reluctantly. He'd meant what he said. She didn't really know him. She wouldn't have been making love with him tonight, but with a memory. And in the morning, she would have hated, if not him, then herself for giving in to temptation. And he would have hated himself for giving in to desire only to satisfy an old hunger.

He knew all about women who were drawn to dangerous men, who craved the excitement, the daring of playing with fire. It was a game with them. They thrilled to the challenge, if not to the specific men who provided it.

He wanted Ashley to desire him, Dillon Ford, not just the idea of rebelling against propriety as she had when she'd asked him to dance at his prom all those years ago.

Oh, how sweet that memory was to him, all the same. It had haunted him all these years. He'd never forgotten the feel of her in his arms, the gentle sway of her body into his, the press of her thighs against his.

Nor had he forgotten how it had felt to know that anything more between them was forbidden, that a girl as good as Ashley was beyond his reach. His pride had taken a beating that night, right along with his libido. Tonight had reminded him a lot of those days, when he'd known he could claim her body, but not her heart.

Despite his earlier promise to himself to steer clear of Trent's favorite Scotch, he poured himself a double on the rocks. Sipping it, he tried to block out the burning humiliation he had suffered for himself and Ashley at the crude remarks he'd overheard that long-ago night after the dance had ended.

One part of him hadn't given a damn, because he'd glimpsed just a little bit of heaven while holding her. Another part had vowed that the next time he and Ashley Wilde came face-to-face it would be as equals. No one would smirk at finding the two of them together. That promise had driven him all these years.

Now here they were, face-to-face and practically a whole lot more, and he'd discovered very little had changed. Back then she might not have thought she was slumming when she'd danced with him, as others had so rudely accused, but after tonight he couldn't help wondering if that was exactly what she thought now. Her doubts were written all over her face every time she looked at him. He suspected once more that she was simply using him as a diversion.

Ironically, in his unique world of high-tech security and discreet protection services, he was every bit as famous as she was in hers. After all, it had been his company she had sought when she'd been troubled by those threats. He wondered what she would think when she discovered that months ago their paths had almost crossed.

At any rate, he had every reason to be as proud of his accomplishments as she was of hers. His was just a less public environment. If balance sheets counted for anything, they were equals and then some.

But confronted with a woman who mattered, he realized that that wasn't nearly enough. He wanted to see her eyes shining with desire, yes. He also wanted to see respect and trust. He told himself that was all the proof he'd ever need that he'd overcome the past—and then he could put Riverton, Wyoming and Ashley Wilde out of his mind forever.

Chapter Seven

When Dillon wandered into the kitchen the following morning wearing a pair of blue jeans and nothing more, he was astounded to find himself facing Mrs. Fawcett's disapproving scowl. Ashley shot him an amused, if somewhat helpless, look over the brim of her coffee mug. He gathered their uninvited guest had been there for some time.

Decked out in another of those appallingly ill-fitting hiking outfits, his old high school math teacher faced him with a prim set to her mouth.

"I might have expected as much," she said. "I knew when I saw the two of you together the other day that you were up to no good." She turned to Ashley. "What would your father say if he knew you were up here with *him?*"

"I'm not *with him,* as you put it," Ashley said, her expression ironic as she met Dillon's gaze.

"Don't split hairs with me," Mrs. Fawcett scolded. "You know exactly what I mean. You're both here under the same roof with no one to keep you out of mischief."

Dillon had poured himself a cup of coffee and taken his first sip when he decided the lecture had gone far enough. He walked over to the table and drew a chair up until he was knee-to-knee with the older woman.

To her credit, she didn't so much as flinch at the deliberately intimidating tactic. Given the difference in their sizes, he assessed her to be one tough cookie. But then, he'd always known that about her. She'd ruled a classroom of unruly teenagers without ever raising her voice.

"Mrs. Fawcett, with all due respect, what goes on under this roof between Ashley and me is none of your business."

Clearly undaunted, she waved a finger under his nose. "Don't take that tone with me, young man. You tangle with me and you'll discover the real meaning of trouble."

"Oh, I'm sure you're a real fireball," he concurred, grinning at her indignation. "But I also suspect that at heart you're a romantic."

The woman who hated gossip looked as horrified as if he'd suggested she peeked at the supermarket tabloids. "Why on earth would you think that?"

He glanced at Ashley and grinned. "I'll bet you remember, don't you?"

Ashley nodded. "The roses," she said at once.

Mrs. Fawcett blushed furiously. "What do some old roses have to do with anything?"

"You tell us," Dillon teased. "They were on your desk every Monday morning both years I was in your class."

"Red," Ashley recalled. "The most incredible shade of red I'd ever seen. A whole dozen of them. You were the envy of every girl in class. We always wondered who'd sent them."

"Pure teenage foolishness," Mrs. Fawcett said. "It was my husband, of course. Who else?"

"How long were you married?" Ashley asked.

"Thirty years."

"And he sent roses all that time?" Dillon asked, his gaze fixed on Ashley. He wondered if she would appreciate a similarly sweet and lavish gesture.

"He started sending me roses at the beginning of every week when we were courting," Mrs. Fawcett revealed. "And he kept it up until the day he died."

"See," Dillon said triumphantly. "That just proves my point about you being a romantic."

"It proves my husband was a romantic, not me," she said, but her eyes were a little misty when she said it and there was a little less snap in her voice. "Besides, that was a long time ago and it doesn't have anything at all to do with the two of you misbehaving."

"I can assure you we are not misbehaving," Dillon said, as Ashley shot another wry look in his direction.

"As if I'd believe anything you said," Mrs. Fawcett declared.

Dillon tried not to take offense at the insult, but it cut just the same. To his surprise, Ashley immediately jumped to his defense.

"It's the truth," she confirmed. "Really, Mrs. Fawcett, Dillon and I mistakenly turned up here at the same time. Rather than one of us being forced to find another place to stay, we decided to share."

"Mighty convenient, if you ask me. I recall how the two of you used to look at each other when you thought no one would catch you. Saw that same gleam in your eyes at the store the other day. That kind of spark leads to no good, I can tell you. That's why I decided it was up to me to make sure everything here is on the up and up, before you do something you'll regret."

"What are you proposing we do about the situation?" Dillon asked.

"One of you could leave," she suggested hopefully. "There must be someplace else one of you could go."

"I'm not leaving," Dillon and Ashley responded in chorus.

That drew Mrs. Fawcett's first glimmer of a smile. "I think I see the problem. You're both too stubborn to give in."

"It's a family trait," Dillon said. "All the Wilde women share it, along with their father."

"You don't have to tell me about Trent Wilde," Mrs. Fawcett said, her expression turning nostalgic. "He was in the very first algebra class I ever taught.

Drove me to distraction, he did. In fact, he did everything he possibly could to make me regret going into teaching at all."

"My father?" Ashley asked, astonishment written all over her face.

"Oh, you've always thought of him as an upright member of this community, and indeed, that is what he became, but back then, let me tell you, he was a hellion."

Ashley's suddenly thoughtful gaze settled on Dillon.

"I know what you're thinking," he said.

Her lips twitched. "Oh, do you really? You can read my mind now, too?"

"It's not all that difficult," he assured her. "You think you've just discovered the key to the friendship between your father and me."

"Mrs. Fawcett's revelations about Daddy do raise some interesting comparisons, I must admit," she said.

The retired math teacher looked vaguely bemused by the twist the conversation had taken. "I must be missing something. Are you saying that this young man and your father are friends?"

"So Dillon assures me," Ashley concurred. "And he did arrive here with the key."

"It's the truth," Dillon insisted, not one bit happy about the mutual skepticism the two were expressing. "Look, I can settle this once and for all. Why don't we call Trent in Arizona and he can vouch for it?"

"No phone," Ashley reminded him.

"I have one," he admitted sheepishly.

She stared at him as if he'd announced he owned stock in a company that sold guns to terrorists.

"You lying, cheating rat," she said, her cheeks flushed with indignation.

"Oh, no, you don't, sweetheart. Don't even go there," he warned. "I never once said I didn't have a phone the other night. I asked where you were going to get your hands on one."

Ashley glowered at him. Mrs. Fawcett merely looked confused.

"What does a phone have to do with anything?"

"Never mind," Dillon told her. "The point is if the two of you don't want to take my word that Trent and I are friends, we can call him and put the matter to rest."

"That is not the issue," Mrs. Fawcett insisted. "It's the impropriety of this arrangement you have here." She stared hard at Dillon again. "And you sitting here half-naked, without thinking twice about it. It tells me I was right to come when I did."

"Believe me, your timing was impeccable," Ashley said. A devilish gleam lit her eyes right before she said, "Perhaps you have a room you'd like to let to Dillon for the remainder of his time in the area."

Dillon choked on his coffee.

"As a matter of fact, I do," Mrs. Fawcett said thoughtfully. "I suppose that would work. There would certainly be no monkey business between you two if he were under my watchful eye." She nodded happily. "Yes, I like it. Pack your things, young man." She directed a meaningful look at his bare chest. "I assume you do have some clothes with you."

Dillon didn't like the way they seemed to be eagerly taking charge of his life. "Excuse me, but I have some say in this, and I am not going anywhere. I made arrangements to borrow Trent's cabin and I intend to stay in Trent's cabin." He scowled at Ashley. "I thought we had settled this days ago."

"A few things have come up since then."

"Such as?" he demanded, wondering if she would dare to mention the previous night's interlude.

She seemed to be struggling for a suitable response. Finally, she said, "People know we're here together now."

"Not people," he pointed out. "Just Mrs. Fawcett, and as you yourself reassured me the other day, Mrs. Fawcett is the epitome of discretion." He stared hard at the teacher. "I'm sure that's true, isn't it?"

The older woman looked torn between her honor and her very clear mission to split the pair of them up.

"Of course, I keep what I know to myself," she finally declared staunchly. "That doesn't mean you should get away with these shenanigans."

"What shenanigans?" Dillon asked. "We've both assured you there are no shenanigans going on."

"Oh, fiddle-faddle," she said dismissively. "Only a fool would believe that, and I'm no fool.

Besides, even if it is true now, it won't be for long. The sparks flying between you two could set the woods on fire. I owe it to Trent to see that nothing comes of that."

"After the way he treated you way back when, you feel you owe him more loyalty than you do us?" Dillon asked.

"He changed," she said, as if that was explanation enough.

"So have I," Dillon said quietly.

But he could tell from the expressions that greeted his announcement there were two women in the room who didn't believe him.

Ashley hadn't been at all sure that Mrs. Fawcett would ever give up and go away without one of them in tow. Eventually, though, she had left alone with the promise that she would be checking on them.

"At any hour of the day or night, so mind your p's and q's," she warned them.

After she had reluctantly left them, Ashley turned to Dillon, whose eyes were sparkling with pure mischief, just as they had all those years ago. "Do you feel like you're sixteen again?" she asked.

"More like twelve," he said.

"Oh, of course," she said. "You were far more precocious than I was."

"Don't sound so regretful about it," he said. "Being precocious wasn't all it's cracked up to be. People tend not to take you very seriously, unless you count the fact that shop owners never take their eyes off you. That was about as serious as a bullet to the chest."

Ashley was surprised by the bitterness in his voice. "Was it that awful?"

"Being tried and judged by every adult in town? It wasn't all that much fun. And if you think the shop owners were bad, you should have seen the looks I got from parents every time I went anywhere close to their daughters." His expression turned rueful. "Of course, they might have had some reason to worry."

"No doubt." She studied him intently as a thought occurred to her for the first time. "Dillon, were you as bad as everyone thought you were?"

"You mean with girls?"

She nodded.

"Sweetheart, I didn't get that reputation by sitting home alone on Saturday nights."

"Amazing."

"What is?"

"That you never got caught."

He looked vaguely uneasy at that, which stirred her suspicions. "You didn't, did you?"

He shook his head, his expression unreadable. If Ashley had had to guess what he was thinking, she would have said he found this question, like so many others, insulting. Even so, he answered it.

"No, you can relax. There are no little Ford babies running around Riverton unclaimed."

She nodded, gratified. "Which brings me back to my original point. If you were so bad, if half the girls in town were so eager to jump into the sack with you, how come you didn't get caught? No one is that lucky. Teenagers make mistakes all the time, especially when they're taking so many chances."

"Maybe I was very careful."

"Or maybe you never slept with any of them," she said, watching closely for his reaction.

"You heard all the talk. You know I did."

She noticed he didn't quite meet her eyes when he said it. "Or was it just girls wanting everyone to believe that they'd conquered the dangerous Dillon Ford?" she speculated.

"Sweetheart, don't you know all that locker-room talk is something only guys do?"

"Obviously, you've never been at a teenage girls' slumber party."

"Well, actually…"

Ashley chuckled. "I should have known. Whose was it?"

"I never, ever kissed and told," he declared piously. "I don't intend to start now."

"Well, your dates certainly did. How much were they making up, Dillon?" she asked again, refusing to let the matter drop until he'd given her a straight answer.

He stood and poured himself another cup of coffee. He took a very long time doing it. A suspicious person might think he was trying to hide something. Ashley had gone beyond suspicion to flat-out conviction.

"How old were you when you made love for the first time?" she asked.

"Isn't that awfully personal?"

"Considering how close we've become, to quote you, I'd say I have a right to ask a few personal questions."

"Can I plead the Fifth?"

"This isn't a court of law."

"It feels like it."

"Dillon, the question isn't all that complicated or particularly damning. Quite the contrary, in fact."

"No, you're just suggesting that I was a fraud back then."

So she was, Ashley realized. "Well, only in the best possible way."

He laughed at that. "Is it any wonder I find you fascinating? You have the most convoluted, twisted logic of any woman I've ever known. Most women try to prove the men they're involved with are sleeping around on them. You're dead certain I wasn't sleeping around ten years ago, when all the evidence points to the contrary."

"What evidence? A bunch of hormonal seventeen-year-olds out to prove how grown-up and daring they were?"

Dillon sighed. "Where were you a decade ago?"

"Trying to figure out how to get on your list of conquests," she admitted candidly.

Pure lust suddenly shimmered in his eyes. "It's never too late."

"So they say," Ashley agreed. "But I want straight answers first."

"Why?"

"Because I can't figure out why you'd let everyone in town believe you were so bad when my guess is that you never touched those girls."

"Oh, I touched a few of them," he confessed, then sighed. "But you're right. It never went any further than that. I was twenty when I made love for the first time."

"Mind-boggling," she said, half to herself. "Then why did you let everyone believe you were so bad?"

"You won't understand."

"Try me."

"Because having a reputation as a juvenile delinquent seemed better to me at seventeen than having no reputation at all."

Ashley struggled with the implications of that for several minutes before conceding defeat. "You're right. I don't understand."

"Why should you?" he said bitterly. "You were the daughter of the most powerful man in town. You were bright and beautiful and just about as close to perfect as a summer sky. You were everyone's role model. Mothers berated their daughters for not being more like you, and fathers berated their sons for not courting you."

Ashley winced at the assessment. "Don't you think that's a bit of an exaggeration?"

"Do you?" he countered.

Ashley sighed. "Okay, I suppose people did think that, but they were all overestimating me. I was just an insecure teenage girl, like all the rest. At any rate, what does that have to do with you?"

"I was a nobody, with a father who wasn't around most of the time and no mother at all," he said.

He said it with surprisingly little resentment. Apparently he'd been saving that for her all these years. She began to wonder if his feelings for her back then had been fascination or antagonism. Based on what he was saying now, she must have represented a lot of things he disliked. She listened intently for some clue as he continued to describe the way it had been for him.

"I had to take on too much responsibility at home too early. My grades were lousy. The first time anybody paid any attention to me was when my best friend at the time shoplifted a pack of gum and I got blamed for it."

"How old were you?"

"Ten, maybe eleven. All of a sudden adults couldn't pay enough attention to me. Even my father took notice for the first time in a long time. I began to see that being bad had its advantages."

"A classic case of acting out to get attention," Ashley said softly, feeling sympathy well up inside her. Dillon's warning look kept her from expressing any hint of the pity she felt for that sad boy.

"By the time I reached high school, it was a habit. I knew right from wrong and I never—well almost never," he corrected with a rueful grin, "crossed that line. But by then everyone had stopped giving me the benefit of the doubt. I'd done everything I could to earn my reputation as a bad kid, and I clung to it because it was all I had."

Ashley thought about a scared, lonely little boy

choosing the wrong path just to get something that she and her sisters had taken for granted—the attention of grown-ups.

"Oh, Dillon," she whispered.

"Don't you dare feel sorry for me," he ordered tightly. "I didn't tell you that story so you would pity me. I told you because you badgered me for the truth. Now you have it." He regarded her intently. "It's not nearly as provocative as thinking I was some sort of bad seed, destined to head straight to hell, is it?"

Ashley was shocked by his assessment. "Meaning what, exactly?"

"That you were like all the others. Still are, for that matter. You were attracted to me because I represented danger and rebellion. If I'd just been another kid in the class getting average or below-average grades, wearing blue jeans and plaid shirts and cowboy boots, you would never have looked at me twice."

"That's not true," Ashley insisted, then thought back to the way she'd been in high school. She'd only dated the best and brightest, never the average or uninteresting. Dillon had been fascinating because he was dangerous and forbidden. She couldn't deny that. "Okay, maybe back then I wouldn't have been as drawn to you."

"And now?"

"Dillon, there's a chemistry between us."

"But how much of that is a carryover from before, from thinking that I'm a little shady and a whole lot dangerous?"

"None of it," she said at once, then sighed, forced into being honest by that penetrating gaze of his. "Okay, maybe some of it. I don't know. How can I, when you have never let anyone get to know the real you?"

"Your father knows me. So do a lot of other people, actually. Of course, I had to move out of Riverton to live down my reputation."

"You could have stayed here and fought it."

He shot her an all-too-knowing look. "Maybe I just wanted to get away and be somebody different. You should understand that better than anyone."

Ashley swallowed hard. "Because I ran away to New York so I could stop being Trent Wilde's perfect daughter," she said.

"Exactly." His sharp-eyed gaze bored into her. "Did it work?"

"Of course, it did," she said at once.

"I'm not talking about the obvious now," he said. "I mean deep down inside, where it counts. Did you find out who Ashley Wilde really is?"

The question was so close to what was troubling her these days that she couldn't even meet his gaze. She realized she didn't like having the tables unexpectedly turned on her. Cross-examining Dillon was one thing. Being subjected to an intensive probing herself was another.

"We were talking about you," she protested swiftly.

He grinned. "Not any more. It's turnabout time. You've been digging around in my psyche for the past hour or so. Now I want to know what makes Ashley Wilde tick."

She regarded him uneasily. "Why? Just to get even?"

"Maybe it's because I care what goes on in that gorgeous head of yours." He waved a finger under her nose. "And don't deny that there's a lot going on, because I'm not buying it anymore. You didn't come up here to get in tune with nature. Every time I gaze into those beautiful eyes of yours I see how troubled you are."

Because she'd had just about all the intense conversation she could handle for one morning and figured he had, too, Ashley opted for resistance to his probing. She tilted her head defiantly. "Who says?"

"I say," Dillon countered, but unexpectedly he relented. "Okay, we'll play it your way for this morning. Let's go fishing."

She wasn't sure that was a big improvement over being analyzed. "I never catch anything," she grumbled.

"Sweetheart, this is one of the few cases where the process is almost as important as the results. Stick with me and I'll teach you how to become laid back and relaxed."

Since she devoutly wished she could relax and find a little serenity, even though she doubted it would be with a fishing pole in hand, she agreed readily. "I'll get the poles."

"And your waders," he said. "None of this sissy stuff, standing on the shore."

"Of course not."

He stood up, moved to her side and leaned down to brush a kiss across her forehead. "First lesson, sweetheart. This is fun. Stop looking as if you've been doomed to a lifetime in the coal mines."

"I'll cheer up when I catch a bigger fish than you do," she countered grimly.

Dillon, blast him, chuckled. "Maybe you'd better settle for just catching any fish at all."

Chapter Eight

The fish were biting—Dillon had thrown back half a dozen—but Ashley couldn't seem to catch one. Dillon watched with amusement as she got more and more frustrated, then annoyed, then grimly determined. At this rate, they'd be standing thigh-deep in the stream until nightfall, he concluded.

"You aren't relaxing," he called out.

She turned a ferocious look on him. "Hell, no, I'm not relaxing. These fish are not going to get the better of me again."

"It's not important," he reminded her. "This is a sport."

"Some sport when a twelve-inch creature can get the better of a human being. We have brains and muscles."

"Don't forget the flies. We have superior flies,"

he reminded her, barely managing to keep a straight face.

She scowled at him. "I'm delighted you find this so amusing. How many fish have you caught?"

"Enough," he assured her, figuring diplomacy called for evasiveness. "We won't starve tonight."

"Meaning two more than I've caught, I suppose. Well, we are not leaving this stream until I've got two fish of my own."

Dillon groaned at the prompt stirring of her pride. "Why didn't I remember how competitive you are? I would have thrown them all back."

"All?" she said ominously. "What do you mean by that? Were there more than two?"

Whoops, Dillon thought. "It doesn't matter."

"It does."

"This isn't about winners and losers," he tried to point out. Since she clearly wasn't convinced, he added a few more philosophical points for good measure. "It's about being a part of nature, being out here in the fresh air, being together. Don't turn it into something competitive."

"I am not the least bit competitive," she declared. "This has nothing to do with you. I have to prove I'm as smart as these damned fish."

"And you think it's better to compete with a fish than with me?" he inquired, unable to keep the irony out of his voice.

"Why not? Men do it all the time." She shot him a look of pure disgust. "Oh, Dillon, for heaven's sake, go sit on the bank and go to sleep. All this talk is scaring the fish away."

He could think of only one way to end this, by giving her a new focus for all that rampaging competitiveness. "Make me," he challenged.

Startled, she turned too quickly and almost slipped. "Excuse me?" she said, when she'd caught her balance.

His blood pumped a little faster, watching that spark of irritation flare in her eyes. Taunting Ashley was far better sport than landing a few fish. She was so darned quick to rise to the bait.

He leveled his gaze straight at her and repeated, "I said if you want me to keep quiet, make me."

Incredulity spread across her face. Fire sparked in her eyes. "You can't just be quiet because it's the proper, respectful thing to do?"

"I am not a proper and respectful man, remember?"

"I thought we'd pretty much destroyed that particular illusion this morning."

"Not so I've noticed," he said. "I still feel very much like stirring up trouble, especially when it comes to you. There's just something about you that makes me want to risk all sorts of dangerous things."

She looked a little nonplussed by that. "And the only way I can keep you quiet would be to...do what?" she asked cautiously.

"That would be up to you," he said graciously. "Be inventive."

She gingerly took a step toward him, picking her way carefully over the slippery rocks. There was a worrisome gleam of deadly intent in her eyes. Dillon backed up a step, mostly to keep the game alive. Ashley's competitive streak did serve its purposes. It promised to keep things between them very interesting.

Ashley never took her gaze off him as she slipped and slid, muttering unladylike oaths under her breath as she drew closer and closer, dragging her fishing rod after her, the line still dangling in the water. Dillon noticed it was suddenly bobbing and weaving in her wake, a sure sign that she'd inadvertently snagged her first catch of the day.

"You've got a fish," he called out.

She didn't even glance over her shoulder. "Very funny," she said dismissively. "If you think I'm buying that, you're crazy. You're just trying to distract me from the dunking I have planned for you."

Just as the words were out of her mouth, the line jerked with a powerful tug that cost her her balance. Before Dillon could move, she'd tumbled head over heels backward into the icy water. He noted, though, that she still had a death grip on that rod. Clearly, she did not intend to let her one and only catch of the day get away.

He splashed closer and held out his hand. "Let me reel it in for you."

"Not on your life. This fish is mine, buster." She scrambled to her feet as she said it, impatiently swiping at locks of soaking wet hair.

Dripping from head to toe, but seemingly oblivious to it, she focused all her intention on getting that fish safely reeled in.

Watching her took his breath away. She was

amazing in her total commitment, her absolute dedication to the task. A woman capable of that degree of absorption would be magnificent in bed. He grew hard just imagining it.

The triumphant expression on her face when the huge silvery trout emerged from the stream certainly indicated she thought the fish was worth the drenching she had taken.

"Nice catch," Dillon observed.

"Bigger than yours?" she demanded at once.

"You never let up, do you?" he said, chuckling. "At first glance, I would have to agree it is bigger than either of my fish." He regarded her quizzically. "Does that mean we can go back to the cabin and get you out of those wet clothes before you get pneumonia? Or do you plan to stay here until you have two fish?"

Even standing there soaked to the skin, she looked torn. Dillon was fairly certain he could tell exactly what she was thinking. After all, this was only one fish and he had caught two, which would make him better in the eyes of some mythical fish counter, he supposed.

All those years of striving for perfection had cost her dearly, apparently. She never knew when to quit. He began to wonder if Trent had been wise to instill such a competitive, determined streak in her. Would she ever be content with anything less than being the best?

When she remained silent, he prodded. "Ashley?"

"I guess we can go back," she finally agreed with obvious reluctance.

Dillon set a grueling pace, hoping that would keep her body temperature up, but by the time they reached the cabin, she was shivering uncontrollably. Dillon rushed inside, grabbed a quilt off his bed and brought it into the living room, where she was standing perfectly still, dripping all over the floor.

"Here, wrap this around you."

She stared at it in a daze. "I'll get it all wet."

"Better that than you freezing to death," he advised as he nudged her toward a chair in front of the fire. Though it was plenty warm in the cabin with the dying embers from last night's fire, he tossed on another log. "Now sit here while I run a hot bath for you. It won't take a minute."

Even with her teeth chattering, she still managed an incredibly seductive expression as she said, "I'd get a whole lot warmer a whole lot faster if you'd just get into the bath with me."

Temptation made his blood roar. "Ashley, I really don't think—"

"Don't think," she advised at once.

"But—"

"Dare you," she said, her gaze locked with his.

Dillon sighed. Resisting temptation was one thing. He'd had a lot of practice at that. But a dare? He never, ever turned down a dare. All those revelations about his motives for allowing himself to look like a bad boy hadn't covered that one point. He truly had thrived on responding to every single outrageous dare ever made to him. When he'd responded to a taunting dare, he'd felt as if he fit in somehow. Living on the edge had become a way of life, only now, with his security firm, he managed to do it within the law.

"That wasn't smart," he said, his voice ragged.

"What wasn't smart?"

"Daring me."

"Who cares about smart?" she insisted. "I want you, and something tells me that is not going to go away just because it might be the sensible thing to do. We ignored whatever this is between us years ago, and if you ask me, all that did was delay the inevitable."

She had a point, Dillon decided as she stood up and let the quilt fall away. She moved slowly toward him.

Even damp and bedraggled, she was irresistible, Dillon thought. When she was close enough, he touched a wet lock of hair that had glued itself to her cheek and gently brushed it away. Even that quick, fleeting contact sent fire shimmering through him. He closed his eyes and mentally battled temptation and his conscience, two contrary forces.

But even as he waged his internal struggle, he felt Ashley's arms circle his neck, felt her breasts skim his chest. He could feel the tight buds of the nipples, stiffened by cold and arousal to a state that made him long to take each one into the warmth of his mouth.

"Has anyone ever mentioned that you don't play fair?" he asked, knowing that this time he was beyond resisting what she was offering. All those noble sentiments he'd expressed the night before had fled, consumed by the fire raging inside him.

"All the time," she said cheerfully. "I am a Wilde, after all."

It was not exactly the reminder that Dillon needed. Thinking of Trent's reaction to an affair between his beloved youngest daughter and Dillon gave Dillon serious pause.

Just as he was thinking that he'd rather ache with longing for the rest of his life than betray his old friend by seducing his daughter, Ashley framed his face with her chilled hands and looked him squarely in the eye.

"This is between you and me, Dillon. My father has nothing to do with it."

So now she was reading his mind, Dillon thought with a sigh. Were there no limits to her ability to twist him inside out?

She touched a finger to his lips, her gaze still fixed on him. "Do you want me? Tell the honest to goodness truth, Dillon. No platitudes or excuses."

There was something in her voice that haunted him. She sounded almost as if she was uttering a desperate plea. That couldn't be, of course. Why would Ashley Wilde have any need at all to beg a man to make love to her? Her conquests were legendary.

Yet gazing into those fascinating, compelling topaz eyes, he saw an astonishing and unexpected vulnerability. He knew, then, that the truth was his only option. "I want you," he admitted. "Always have."

"Then that's all that matters."

She said it with such confidence that he had to believe her, wanted desperately to believe her because a moment he'd dreamed of forever finally seemed to be within reach. The secretive, Mona Lisa smile that bloomed on her face reassured him, but he had to be sure.

"You are absolutely positive you know what you're doing?" he demanded one last time. "That dip in the stream didn't freeze your brain cells?"

"My brain cells are perfectly fine, thank you very much. But the rest of me would like to get into a hot bath."

He shrugged off his doubts and scooped her into his arms. "Then what else can I do but oblige," he said as he carried her down the hall to the master bath where everything was oversize to accommodate precisely the sort of provocative intimacy they had in mind.

"For once, I am very glad that your father thought of everything," he observed as he set her on her feet long enough to turn on the water and add a handful of bath salts that promptly mounded into shimmering bubbles.

As the water splashed into the gigantic tub, Dillon turned his attention to Ashley. Fingers shaking, she was fiddling ineptly with the buttons of her blouse. He shoved her hands aside and completed the job himself, forcing himself not to linger in the interests of getting her into that tub and warmed up in a hurry.

"You've had lots of practice at that, I see," she said.

Dillon refused to rise to the bait. "I've been unbuttoning my own shirts for years," he agreed as he continued stripping away sopping wet clothes until she was completely, gloriously nude.

He wanted to take his time examining her from head to toe, drinking in the sight of her, but now was not the time. It took everything in him to do the noble thing and put aside his yearnings.

"That's not what I meant, and you know it," she said, seemingly oblivious to her state of total undress and its potent effect on him.

He grinned. "Yes, I do, but this bathroom will be awfully crowded if you want to start bringing in old flames. And don't forget, if mine come in, so do yours. And I have lots of old tabloid headlines as ammunition."

She nodded. "Good point." She batted her eyelashes at him in exaggerated flirtatiousness. "So, it's just you and me, then?"

"Two has always seemed to be an appropriate number, don't you think? Adam and Eve. All those creatures on the ark. Romeo and Juliet."

She glanced around at all the marble, which was in stark contrast to the rest of the cabin's rough-hewn logs. "Do you think any of them had accommodations this luxurious?"

"They probably thought so," he said. "Besides, they were no doubt a whole lot more fascinated with each other than with their surroundings." No longer able to resist, he skimmed the tip of his finger over bare skin that was still covered with goose bumps. "The same way I am with you."

She gave a quick, startled glance at her naked body. "Even though I'm shivering so badly, I look a little like a plucked chicken?"

"Sweetheart, there is not even the remotest resemblance between you and a chicken. You can trust me on that one."

Grabbing a towel from the heated rack, he rubbed her skin briskly until it was warm and turning pink again. "See, smooth and beautiful, just like satin."

The gesture and the light tone cost him, though. His pulse was throbbing so fast and furiously he was sure he was no more than one step away from a major cardiac incident.

Ashley's eyes lit with fire and an impudent gleam that struck him as slightly worrisome.

"Ash?"

"Sssh," she whispered. "It's my turn. I have to get you out of these clothes before all that water turns cold."

Though she fumbled more than once, her dedication to the task of stripping him was apparent. She had his shirt off and his pants unzipped before Dillon could catch his breath. When her fingers skimmed over his arousal, he thought he'd died and gone straight to heaven.

Unfortunately, though, it was a dangerous game she was playing. "I think you've had enough fun for the moment," he told her, gently shoving aside her inquisitive fingers. He shucked off pants and briefs and took a quick step into the tub.

"Perfect," he assessed and held out his hand. "Join me?"

Gaze and hands locked with his, Ashley stepped gracefully into the water and slid down, tugging him down opposite her so they were sitting face-to-face. Their legs tangled intimately.

Buoyed by the seductive sway of the neck-deep sudsy water, Ashley leaned against the edge of the tub and closed her eyes. With a layer of bubbles foaming provocatively over her pink skin, with the peaks of her breasts playing hide-and-seek in the gentle waves caused by the slightest movement, she could have tormented a stronger man than Dillon into forgetting every resolution he'd ever made. He wanted her with a fierce urgency that drove out common sense and just about everything else.

"Warmer now?" he asked, his voice choked in his battle to move ahead slowly. He vowed he would let her back out at any point along the way, no matter what it cost him.

"Luxuriously so," she murmured, sounding half asleep.

He might have thought he was going to lose her to sleep if it hadn't been for the slow, deliberate slide of her foot along his calf. He swallowed hard and tried to focus on counting the tiles above the tub. He made it to thirty-six before succumbing totally to sensation.

"Another ten seconds of that and I'll have you out of here and into bed before you know it," he warned in a deceptively lazy tone.

"Really?"

She sounded more fascinated than scared. Dillon scowled as she stretched until her toes skimmed yet another part of his anatomy, which reacted with predictable swiftness. Judging by her expression, she was quite pleased with herself.

"You just don't get it, do you?" he muttered with mock ferocity.

"Oh, yes, I do," she said cheerfully.

"In other words, you are deliberately provoking me?"

"I certainly hope so."

"Were you this impudent in high school?"

"Of course," she said breezily. "That's why you were as fascinated with me as I was with you. We were soul mates. Two of a kind. A matching set."

Dillon chuckled. "I get the picture. Unfortunately, as we've already discussed, it was based on a misapprehension on your part. Still is, for that matter."

"Don't go spoiling it for me," she scolded. "The image of you dressed all in black riding that Harley has kept me going for years now. You looked very bad."

"You of all people must know that looks can be deceiving. You look like an angel with all that blond hair cascading to your shoulders and your skin all pink and glowing from this steamy water. And yet your behavior..." He glanced meaningfully at her toes, which were doing their inventive best to drive him completely crazy.

She grinned at the implications of that. "Which still makes us polar opposites. If I'm the real brat here and you're the saint..."

"I never said I was a saint."

"Don't split hairs. I'm on a roll here. The bottom line is we're still opposites, we still attract."

"You'll get no argument from me on that score," he said, then groaned as her toes hit their mark yet again. Enough was definitely enough.

With a movement so quick she had no time to react with anything more than a squeal, he tucked his hands under her arms and lifted her out of the water, then settled her on top of him, sending water splashing out of the tub.

The slip-sliding of flesh against flesh stirred enough heat to warm the cooling bathwater all over again. With Ashley's face just above his own, he met her gaze. "Playtime is over, sweetheart."

She sighed as a half smile tugged at her lush pink lips. "It's about time," she murmured as she lowered her head until their lips touched.

Dillon couldn't argue with that. He felt as if he'd been waiting a lifetime for just this moment.

Ashley had never felt so exquisitely sensual in her entire life. With Dillon's naked, aroused body under her own, with warm water lapping gently at their skin, she felt as if she was in the middle of every sexy, romantic scene she'd ever seen in the movies. An image of Burt Lancaster and Deborah Kerr tangled heatedly together on the sand as waves crashed around them came immediately to mind.

The slow, deliberate slide of Dillon's hands over her hips made her heart race. When he touched her already sensitive nipple with his tongue, a fire blazed to life low in her belly. The hard press of his arousal against her thigh teased and taunted. She ached to feel him inside her, to know the magical wonder of truly making love with him after wanting him for so terribly, terribly long.

Okay, maybe her teenage yearnings had been all about rebellion and daring. Maybe this hunger to be united with him still had its roots in rebellion. She didn't know, didn't care. All she knew for certain was that she craved the intense feelings he stirred in her. She needed to feel special and desired. She needed to recapture the sense that she was someone, that she was special, that she was perfect.

She had lost all that in one cutting conversation with her agent. Dillon remembered, though, and he had started to give it back with one heated glance. Now, in his arms, she felt whole again. She felt like the Ashley Wilde who could triumph over anything.

Her insecurities of the night before seemed to have vanished. She had taken an incredible risk earlier, practically begging him to make love to her, but she had known deep inside with a woman's intuitive confidence that this time he wouldn't refuse, that he couldn't walk away a second time.

It didn't matter that the real problem hadn't gone away. She wasn't instantly thinner. She wasn't magically cured of all the doubts and insecurities. She knew the path ahead of her was still uncertain, her future plans clouded.

But at this moment, she could push that aside for the incredible sensation of feeling like a desirable woman again. If nothing more ever happened between her and Dillon, if he walked out of her life and never looked back, he still would have given her that. He would have reminded her that the way she felt about herself could be communicated to others. If she felt sexy and wanton, then she was. Dillon had detected the difference in her at once and responded to it. That was all the proof she would ever need that she could control her own destiny, at least in matters of the heart.

Satisfied by this discovery, she closed her eyes and gave herself up to the wild stirrings of her body, the more and more intense caresses that left passionate yearnings in their wake.

Just when she felt her body reaching the edge of a mind-blowing climax, Dillon's touch retreated.

"I am not making love to you for the first time in a bathtub," he said, his voice tight and ragged with the same sort of raw hunger Ashley was feeling.

With surprising agility, he rose in one graceful movement, Ashley cradled in his arms. He carried her into the bedroom and gently lowered her to the bed. She couldn't recall a time when she had ever felt more cherished.

In bed, the sensual assault began again with lingering caresses and slow, deep kisses.

For a man she'd always assumed would be demanding and dangerous in bed, Dillon was astonishingly gentle. Yet there was no mistaking the urgency of his desire or the possessiveness behind his claiming. He made every inch of her his with a stroke of his finger or the brush of his lips.

And when she was quivering with need of her

own, he slid into her oh-so-slowly, filling her, then retreating and filling her again until in a spectacular explosion of sensation, he made her totally, everlastingly his.

Chapter Nine

"Poor old Mrs. Fawcett should see us now," Dillon said as Ashley stretched luxuriously beside him.

"Are you kidding? She'd burn up the phone lines trying to find my father." Apparently feeling emboldened by what they had just shared, she lifted herself until she was sitting astride him, then gazed into his eyes. "And I for one am not interested in being joined up here by him."

"Ditto," Dillon said, trying to ignore the provocative sensations that were already slamming through him again. To his deep regret, making love to Ashley hadn't gotten her out of his system. He feared he might be well and truly hooked. "But we should talk about what just happened here."

"Why? We're two adults. We both knew exactly what we were doing."

"Did we? How would you describe it?"

"We made love." Her expression faltered ever so slightly. "Didn't we?"

"I did."

"You say that as if you're not so certain that's what I did."

Dillon hated to ruin a perfectly incredible afternoon, but he wanted things to be very clear between them. Whatever had drawn Ashley to this hideout hadn't magically gone away. It would be terrific if he could be part of the solution, but he sure as hell didn't want to become part of the problem.

"I'm not certain," he agreed.

"Dillon, I don't do things like this every day. That should tell you something."

"It tells me you wanted me, that for today, at least, you needed me. It doesn't give me a single clue about what's really going on in that brilliant head of yours, though. For all I know you may be on the rebound. You may be using me as a way to mend a broken heart."

She was shaking her head adamantly before he finished. "No, this had nothing to do with another man. You can trust me on that."

"Okay. But you were using me, you were trying to prove something."

She rolled away from him and gathered a sheet around herself. "Look, I'm sorry if I did something wrong, if this didn't work for you," she said, tears brimming in her eyes.

Dillon promptly felt like the worst possible kind of a jerk. Kneeling in front of her, he framed her face with his hands. He brushed her tears away with his thumbs. She trembled at his touch.

"Sweetheart, I assure you there was nothing wrong with anything that happened here. *Nothing,*" he repeated emphatically. "But I need to know why it happened. I've been here with you for days now. I've seen something in your eyes I've never seen before. You're vulnerable. I don't want to think I've taken advantage of that."

"You haven't."

He wasn't reassured. "Then, please, tell me what this was all about."

Even though her lips quivered, they began to tilt into a smile. "Do you realize that thousands and thousands of men and women hop into bed together every single day and they don't need explanations?"

"No-fault sex?" he suggested. "Sorry, sweetheart, but despite popular opinion of my sorry reputation, it doesn't work that way for me. When I sleep with a woman, it means something. The potential consequences are too great for it not to."

Her eyes widened. "You mean…oh, my gosh, we didn't…I could be…"

Dillon nodded. "The last thing I expected when I came up here was to find you waiting for me. From the minute I saw you, I knew we'd be together sooner or later, but I didn't expect it this soon or I would have hightailed it into Riverton for some protection."

He brushed her hair from her face. "You don't need to worry about most of the possible consequences, but there is a chance you could get pregnant. If that happens, no matter where you are or where I am when you find out, I want to know. Understood?''

Ashley swallowed hard, looking vaguely thunderstruck.

''Ashley?''

''I'll tell you. I promise,'' she whispered eventually. She sighed. ''As rebellions go, this one was a doozy, wasn't it?''

So, Dillon thought, he finally had his answer. She had admitted what he had only guessed before—that making love with him had been no more than a long-delayed rebellion. Riverton High's Miss Perfect had slept with the school delinquent. Hallelujah and amen!

And even though he knew more about rebellion than most people learned in a lifetime, even though he'd embraced it as a life-style for a very long time, discovering that it was the only motive behind the most incredible lovemaking of his life hurt like hell.

He looked at Ashley and his heart ached. Suddenly he couldn't bear it a second longer. He brushed a lingering kiss across her forehead, gathered up his clothes and took off.

It was ironic, he thought as he rode off. He had come to Trent's cabin because it was a place where he had always been able to think clearly. Now it was the last place on earth he could gather so much as a coherent thought.

Ashley wasn't entirely sure when she realized Dillon's mood had taken a nosedive and that she was in some way responsible for it.

She went over their heart-stoppingly beautiful afternoon detail by detail. She recalled his demand that she tell him if she discovered she was pregnant.

Then, only moments later, he'd climbed out of the bed they had shared, tugged on his clothes and disappeared without a word. She'd heard the roar of the Harley shortly thereafter. She hadn't seen him since.

It was now well past nightfall, and she was beginning to worry that he'd taken off for good. She couldn't help wondering if he'd simply gotten what he wanted from her and seen no reason to hang around any longer. That would certainly be par for the course with the downhill skid of the rest of her life these days.

How could she have foolishly gotten the idea that there was something special between them? Maybe Dillon was just like everyone else in the world, after all, eager to grab whatever was offered without any thought to giving anything back.

Her snake of an agent had certainly operated under that particular code of ethics, if you could call it ethical to bad-mouth a client the minute there was a dip in the demand for her services.

For all she knew, Dillon was just like him. What did she really know about the man he'd become? Nothing. She didn't even know exactly why he'd come to the cabin in the first place or why he had hung around after discovering her there. His hints about stress could have meant anything.

Ignoring the glimmer of hurt she had detected in

his eyes, she was swept away once more by confusion. All her doubts about his past surged to life again, along with even deeper uncertainties about his motives toward her. He might have been hanging around just to irritate her. Or maybe he had no place else to go.

Despite his denial that he was in trouble with the law, she had no idea if he was in the sort of trouble he used to thrive on getting into. Maybe he'd never broken any major laws, but he'd certainly wandered into some gray areas. Since he was disgustingly silent on the subject of his life, she had to wonder what he wasn't telling her. At the same time, he seemed perfectly content to let her think whatever she wanted to about him.

As lonely and bereft as she'd felt when she'd fled to Wyoming, she'd been all too grateful for his presence. She got some credit for asking pointed questions, but clearly lost when it came to accepting evasive answers. It was possible that she had been incredibly foolish. She'd been so quick to look forward to their lazy walks and late-into-the-night conversations that she'd pushed aside her doubts about him.

Now that she thought about it, she realized they had rarely talked about anything of consequence. Arguments about the most romantic destinations in the world were about as heavy as the conversations had gotten. Dillon had traveled to an impressive number of exotic places for a man who'd left Riverton with little more than the clothes on his back.

Sitting all alone in the bed they had just shared,

she let her imagination run wild. Perversely, thinking of him as some sort of international art or jewel thief gave her an odd thrill. She'd always wanted to do something totally rebellious. Maybe she was finally living on the edge of danger. If he'd only talked about his exploits, she could have experienced his world vicariously.

At least thinking about Dillon's potential list of sins had kept her from having to do any serious soul-searching about her own life. Even if he never came back, she supposed she owed him for providing that distraction.

At the sound of an engine, her spirits quickly soared. So much for listening to her head's doubts rather than her heart's certainties. All that really mattered, it seemed, was that he had come back, after all. The past hour's moping had been over nothing. Clearly, she was losing it if she couldn't even spend a few minutes alone without thinking the worst.

Hopping out of bed and yanking on a robe, she forced herself not to race for the door. In the living room, she chose a spot in front of the fire to wait, listening for the sound of his footsteps on the porch.

His approach, though, was astonishingly quiet, his tread surprisingly light. When an equally light, rapid tap came on the door, her heart leapt into her throat. So, it wasn't Dillon after all.

Biting back disappointment, she opened the door to find Dani standing there, her expression a mix of relief and concern. She gave a quick nod of satisfaction. "So you are here. I thought as much. May I come in?"

Ashley sighed and reluctantly stepped out of her sister's way. "How did you find me?"

"Process of elimination. I started in New York and worked my way west." She studied Ashley with a big sister's quick but thorough appraisal. "Your agent says you fired him. Care to tell me what that's all about? Or why you're moping around here in your bathrobe at five in the afternoon?"

A blush crept up her cheeks. "No," Ashley declared firmly on both counts. "Would you like some tea?"

"I'd prefer some answers, actually."

"Dani, I love you dearly, but you are my sister, not my mother. Stop fussing over me."

Dani sighed heavily. "Is that why you left Three-Stars, because I was hovering? That's what Sara said. She told me I drove you away with all my questions. I'm sorry if I was responsible for you leaving."

Ashley smiled ruefully. "You don't have to feel guilty. Actually, I left because you're clairvoyant. You see straight through me."

"I see. What is it you didn't want me to figure out?"

She knew her sister well enough to realize that this was only the beginning. Despite her momentary contrition, Dani would nag and push until she learned all Ashley's secrets. Ashley's only hope was to delay the process.

"Could we talk about this later?" she pleaded.

"I'm starved. Even if you don't want some tea, I do. I haven't eaten since breakfast." She headed for the kitchen, leaving Dani to trail along after her.

Once she'd convinced her sister that there would be no conversation without food, Dani's nurturing nature kicked in. She stepped in and took over, briskly putting together thick sandwiches and brewing a pot of herbal tea while Ashley retreated to the table.

This was the way it had always been among the three sisters, Ashley recalled, relaxing at last. Dani's maternal instincts had made her the mother hen. Sara and Ashley had balked at the perceived interference, yet they had loved their big sister for caring so passionately.

It was about time Dani had a brood of her own to flutter over, Ashley decided.

"Heard anything from Daddy?" she asked, rather than bringing up what she really wanted to discuss—her sister's marital status. Dani caught enough grief on that subject from their father. He'd been trying to marry her off to some rancher friend of his for years. Balking at that had been the most sensible thing Dani had ever done, even if it had cost her the kids she wanted so desperately to have.

"He's cut a wide swath through Phoenix and Scottsdale," Dani said as she put their food on the table. "He says there's no one there except a bunch of people sitting in the sun and waiting to die."

"I thought that was why he went there," Ashley said. "I thought that was his idea of relaxing."

"No, actually when he left he said he wanted to

kick up his heels. I expect him to venture to L.A. or Vegas one of these days and come home with some twenty-five-year-old with a cowboy fixation.''

''God forbid,'' Ashley said with heartfelt horror.

''We can't make choices for the ones we love,'' Dani pointed out dutifully.

''I'm glad you said that,'' Ashley chimed in. ''Maybe that philosophy will keep your nose out of my business.''

''Nice try,'' her sister said briskly. ''But I'm not so easily dissuaded, especially when you're hiding out up here in a place you always claimed to abhor.''

''No, that was you. I don't even give this cabin much thought.''

''But it was the first place you could think of to run to. Why is that?''

''Because I figured no one would think to look for me here,'' she said pointedly. ''Especially you, given the way you shudder at the mention of it. I wanted to be alone.''

Danielle Marie Wilde was not used to taking hints. It seemed unlikely she would start now. The grim, determined set of her lips confirmed that.

''When you give me the answers I want, then you can be alone,'' she said. ''Sometimes it actually does help to talk, you know.''

Ashley scowled at her. ''Fine, let's talk, then. I swore just two minutes ago that I wasn't going to bring this up, but I can't help it. When are you going to find yourself some decent, loving man and have a passel of kids to worry about?''

Dani merely smiled at that. "Do you honestly think that will get me off your case?"

"I can always hope."

"It won't," she assured her. "Being born my baby sister came with a guarantee. You get a lifetime of me worrying about you. That won't stop no matter how many kids I have, not that there's time left for me to have too many."

"Dani, you are barely thirty years old. You can have all the kids you want. You just have to find the right man."

"Riverton is not exactly crawling with candidates," she said with an air of resignation. "Look, can we stick to the subject? We were talking about you."

"You were," Ashley reminded her. "I was talking about you. I don't like that despondent tone I heard in your voice. Since when do you give up?"

"Hold your questions, little sister. I'm older. I get to go first. Why did you fire your agent?"

Ashley gave up. Keeping the whole thing bottled up inside hadn't accomplished anything. Nor had the flirtation with Dillon distracted her permanently from her own problems. Maybe telling Dani would help. At least she could be certain of a sympathetic shoulder to cry on.

Maybe it was time she had someone in her corner, someone who was blindly loyal or who, at the very least, would sugarcoat the truth so it was bearable.

She drew in a deep breath, then blurted, "I fired him because he said I was too fat for him to get me work."

Dani's mouth gaped with satisfying incredulity. "You're kidding, aren't you?"

"I am not kidding," Ashley assured her flatly.

"You, fat? You could eat nothing but cheesecake for a solid month and still not be fat."

Ashley's eyes swam with tears. "Thank you for saying that."

"I am not just saying it," Dani insisted, jumping up and beginning to pace. It was a sure sign of her level of agitation.

"It's the truth," she swore. "Of all the most ridiculous, addlepated notions I have ever heard, this one surely takes the cake. You shouldn't have fired the jerk. You should have shot him."

She said it so fiercely, Ashley was glad that her agent was safely tucked away in New York. She would have hated to see her sister jailed for killing the man. He wasn't worth it.

"Look, it's no big thing," she swore, grasping for a positive spin to settle her sister down. "There are other agents. And I'll probably lose these couple of extra pounds with a little effort. I'll be back in the business in no time."

"You don't sound very enthusiastic about the prospect," Dani observed, cutting right to the heart of Ashley's dilemma.

Ashley's bravado wilted. "That's just it. It doesn't seem to matter so much anymore. But who am I, if I'm not Ashley Wilde, world-famous cover model?"

Dani's expression turned thoughtful. "It's a funny thing about expectations, isn't it?" she said quietly.

"We grow up with one set and the next thing you know they're in tatters and we're left floundering around for some new role for ourselves."

There was no mistaking the fact that the comment had as much to do with her own life as it did with Ashley's. Nor was there any mistaking the sadness in her brown eyes. It was so rare to see her older sister anything but cheerful and determined that Ashley was taken aback. Dani always presented such a serene front to the world that it was difficult to realize she was susceptible to bouts of depression, too.

Ashley rushed over to hug her tightly. "It's going to work out for both of us," she promised.

Dani hugged her back fiercely and managed a watery grin. "Some job of cheering you up, huh? The next thing I know, you're wiping away my tears. I'm sorry. I don't know what came over me."

"Don't worry about it. At least you didn't let Daddy see you all teary-eyed. He'd call the preacher and force you to marry old Roger or Wayne or some other ancient geezer with whom he'd struck up a conversation in Arizona."

Suddenly Dani's expression brightened almost imperceptibly. "Speaking of marriage and men, whose shirt is that?" she asked, gesturing across the room.

Ashley swallowed hard and gazed quickly around the living room for telltale evidence of Dillon's presence. "What shirt?" she inquired blithely, though the T-shirt was unmistakable.

"The faded, well-worn black one, tossed over the

chair. I've certainly never seen you in black, unless it was some skimpy little designer dress in a magazine ad. Besides, this one looks much too large to be yours, and you tend to toss things out before they ever fade that badly."

"I bought it a long time ago to use as a nightshirt," Ashley suggested, frantically grasping at straws.

Dani rolled her gaze heavenward at the blatant fib. She strolled over and picked it up. After a quick sniff, she said, "You're wearing men's cologne now, too? You might be able to fool somebody else with that fiddle-faddle, but not me. Whose is it?"

"Let's just say it belongs to a friend and leave it at that," Ashley pleaded.

"Is this friend helping you to put things into perspective?"

Ashley thought of Dillon's ability to turn her emotions upside down, but she nodded anyway. An analysis of her relationship with Dillon was the last thing she needed right now.

"He's helping," she assured her older sister.

Apparently satisfied with the response, Dani relented. "Then I'll leave it alone for now. Bring him by for a visit when you decide you've had enough of this place, okay?"

Dani glanced around the very masculine cabin and shuddered visibly. "I've already been here longer than I vowed to be ever again."

"Then run along before I suggest we go fishing," Ashley teased. Her expression sobered. "Thanks for coming, though. Talking helped."

"If you came to town, we could do even more of it."

This time Ashley shuddered. "Sorry, big sister. It didn't help that much."

"Whatever decision you reach, you won't leave town without saying goodbye, will you?"

"No, absolutely not."

Dani hugged her, her expression fiercely protective. "I love you. So do Daddy and Sara. Maybe it's time you learned to love yourself."

Ashley sighed. "That is the big trick, isn't it?"

She stood on the porch and watched her sister drive away, dreading the night that stretched out in front of her. Dillon's presence had kept the loneliness and dark thoughts at bay. Without him there, all she had left was the promise of endless hours to think. The prospect depressed her.

She sank into a chair on the porch and tugged her robe more tightly around her to ward off the chill. Before she could get too distraught over the emptiness of the cabin, she heard the sound of another engine. This time it was unmistakably the roar of the Harley.

The joy that spread through her was so intense it stunned her. That alone should have been a danger signal, but she ignored it as she watched Dillon push the Harley off the driveway into a secluded nook in the woods, then stroll toward her with that lazy, seductive gait that had made many a teenage girl weak with longing.

He propped one foot on the bottom step of the porch and gazed at her. "Miss me?"

"Some," she admitted with a deliberately casual shrug. "Where'd you go?"

"For a ride and then into town."

She stared at him, surprised. "You went all the way into Riverton? Why?"

He held a large bag out to her. "See for yourself."

Ashley took the bag, which was surprisingly light considering its size, and peered inside. It was filled with boxes of condoms of every size, texture and color imaginable.

"My, my," she murmured appreciatively. "This looks promising."

"I figured if you were going to have your way with me again and again, I'd better be prepared."

Relief spilled through her. Ashley flew out of the chair and propelled herself straight into his arms with so much force it was a wonder they didn't land in the dirt.

"That's the best present anyone has ever given me," she declared.

"Even better than that candy-red convertible your father gave you for your sixteenth birthday?" he asked doubtfully.

"Better than that."

He grinned. "What was the first thing you did when you got that car?"

Puzzled, she tried to think back. "Turned it on and took it for a test drive," she recalled.

"Care to do the same thing now?" he inquired lightly.

Ashley chuckled at the hopeful gleam in his eyes. "Think I can?"

"Sweetheart, you can turn me on with the blink of an eye."

"Then you'll be absolutely amazed what I can do when I set my mind to it," she promised.

"I can hardly wait."

Chapter Ten

They had made love, slipped out of bed long enough to make themselves a feast of fruit and cheese and crackers, then made love again. Dillon was absolutely, totally spent.

Sprawled across the bed, he wondered if he'd ever be able to move another muscle. No other woman had ever left him feeling so completely and thoroughly satiated, yet still enthralled and wondering what was next. He had fought off his earlier dismay during the ride into Riverton and decided to take whatever happened between them as it came. The past few hours, however, had been beyond even his wildest expectations.

"I think this kind next," Ashley said, holding up two brightly colored condoms. "What do you think? Hot pink or electric blue?"

"I think I made a mistake bringing all those choices home," he said with deliberately feigned exhaustion. "We don't have to sample all of them right away, you know."

The grin that spread across Ashley's face was part arrogance, part feminine delight. "Have I worn you out?" she inquired with exaggerated sympathy.

"Just temporarily, I assure you."

"How temporarily?" she inquired as she did some very inventive checking. Her grin broadened. "Very temporarily, I guess."

"Amazing," Dillon said. "I surprise myself."

"Not me. I always knew you were the sexiest male on the planet."

"And you knew that when you were what?" he inquired dryly. "Sixteen? Seventeen? Was I terribly mistaken about you? Did you have much experience then?"

She winked. "There are some things a woman just knows at any age."

"Well, Ms. Know-It-All, I'll bet I could still teach you a thing or two," Dillon commented.

Instantly fascinated, she asked, "Such as?"

"Oh, no, you don't," he told her. "I'm not giving away all my secrets in just one night. You'll have to be patient, sweetheart."

"How dull."

"But ultimately rewarding," he promised. "Now come up here, stretch out by me and put your head on my shoulder."

When she'd done that and curled her body snugly into his, he sighed. "Perfect."

She stiffened slightly. "There's no such thing," she told him in an oddly tight voice.

He found the reaction worrisome, but Dillon refused to be drawn into some heavy philosophical discussion about perfection in the middle of the night. "If there's not," he said, "then this is the closest thing to it."

Ashley relaxed slightly and sighed, her breath feathering over his bare skin. "It is, isn't it?"

They slept until dawn. Dillon woke first and gazed at the woman sleeping next to him. Her skin was flushed, her hair tangled, but he thought he'd never seen anything so exquisite in all his life. It was no wonder advertising executives courted her to tout their products. She could have sold Satan on turning over a new leaf.

Of course, he knew there was a lot more to Ashley than a pretty face and gorgeous body. With all those Wilde genes rampaging through her, she was bright and spirited and, yes, competitive.

Until he'd found her again, Dillon hadn't realized how desperately he craved that precise combination of attributes in a woman. She represented the kind of challenge that few men dared take on. Dillon was confident enough to believe he was an even match for her. They would be an indomitable pair.

He worried, though, about what her reaction would be if he proposed a more serious relationship than this fleeting fling in a Wyoming cabin. Here, they were both far away from the lives they led. And Ashley still clearly believed that he was bad news, not the kind of man she could ever see herself marrying, no doubt. This was her rebellion, or at least that seemed to be what she was telling herself to justify their impulsive and unexpected relationship.

He wondered, in fact, if she was any more prepared to consider a lasting relationship now than she had been years ago. As he recalled, every boy in their high school had envisioned a future with her, and she'd left them all in the dust as she'd fled to her independent life in New York. She'd left behind a lot of broken hearts and shattered expectations.

He told himself it didn't matter. All he wanted was a fling, wasn't it? Now he'd had that. He should be ready to walk away. But he wasn't. He wanted something more, but time was running out. He only had a few more days before he had to go back to Los Angeles and his real life. Should he ask her to come with him? Would she even consider it? He glanced over and saw that she was awake and watching him with hooded eyes.

"What's wrong?" she asked at once.

He forced a smile. "Why would you think something was wrong?"

"Because you were frowning."

He rolled over and brushed a kiss across her lips. "Maybe I was just frowning because I was lonely for you."

"Then that is definitely a problem I can solve," she said, circling her arms around his neck and proving it.

When they were like this, Dillon thought, nothing at all seemed to matter except the two of them. He wondered if he was only fooling himself, though, to think he could make it last away from this magical place.

It was noon before they finally made it out of bed. Ashley refused to let Dillon anywhere near the tub while she was in it. "That's what got us in trouble in the first place."

"And that would be my fault?" he teased.

"No, I take full responsibility," she agreed. "Or at least partial responsibility. Now go away. If you want to do something useful, fix breakfast."

"Don't you mean lunch?"

"As long as it's edible, I don't care what you call it. And if there's a vegetable involved, keep it to yourself."

"Another rebellion?"

"Perhaps."

Dillon regarded her quizzically but didn't press for an explanation. It was evident from his expression that he recognized there was something behind all these rebellions, small and large. Apparently, though, he'd concluded he'd never figure out what until she was ready to explain. She was grateful for the reprieve.

After casting one last longing look her way, he left the bathroom reluctantly. Ashley heard him whistling as he headed for the kitchen.

She found him there when she'd dressed. He looked thoroughly at home banging pots and pans around, a towel tucked into his pants in lieu of an apron, his chest and feet bare. She envied him his confidence in his body. Despite the past few days, she was still at odds with her own.

"Something smells wonderful," she said, sniffing appreciatively as she wrapped her arms around his waist from behind. "What is it?"

"A secret recipe."

"You won't tell me?"

"Nope. I figure if you like it well enough, you'll follow me anywhere for more."

Ashley peered over his shoulder into the skillet to see what was in there. "Looks like an omelet to me."

"But not just any omelet," he protested with the pride of an artist in his voice. "Sit down."

The distant tinkling of a bell startled them both.

"What on earth?" Ashley asked, just as Dillon muttered an oath under his breath.

"It's my phone."

"Ah, yes, the mysterious cellular phone. Where'd you hide it?"

"It's in my gym bag."

Since he didn't seem to be moving, she asked, "Don't you think you should answer it?"

"Only two people would dare to call me here. I don't want to talk to either one of them."

"Would one of them happen to be my father?"

"You've got it."

"And the other?"

"No one you know," he said tersely.

"A woman?"

"Yes."

"Oh," she said flatly.

"But not a woman friend," he pointed out hurriedly. "She works for me."

"Oh, really," she said, instantly fascinated. "You have an employee?"

"Several, as a matter of fact," he said, avoiding her gaze. His entire attention seemed to be focused on that blasted omelet as the phone kept on ringing. It stopped for an instant, then picked up again.

"Whoever it is is awfully persistent," she observed. "Maybe it's an emergency."

He faced her slowly. "Do you want to answer it so you can satisfy your curiosity?"

Something in his voice warned her that the right answer definitely wasn't yes. "No," she said dutifully.

His harsh expression vanished as he grinned. "Liar."

"Okay, so I want to answer it," she admitted. "Shoot me. I can't stand a ringing phone."

"Maybe you ought to analyze why that's so," he suggested.

"Probably because I was dependent on phone calls for my livelihood."

"Was?"

Ashley nearly groaned at the slip of her tongue. Naturally Dillon had seized on it. Why couldn't he be the sort of man who never paid attention to a word a woman said?

"We were talking about your phone call, not my career," she reminded him. The ringing continued insistently. "Oh, to hell with it, I can't stand it anymore. Unless you forbid it, I'm going to answer it."

She stole a covert glance to gauge his reaction. He seemed totally disinterested in her decision. Apparently he had nothing to hide. He seemed more concerned about the outside world intruding on their time together.

"Dillon?" she pressed.

He shrugged. "Suit yourself. Of course, if it is your father, you will be stirring up one heck of a hornet's nest. Be prepared for the inquisition."

"I can handle my father," she said confidently and ran down the hall to the guest room. She found the cell phone tucked into Dillon's gym bag, just as he'd told her. She snatched it up eagerly.

"Hello."

"Who the hell is this?" a blustery male voice demanded.

No doubt about who was on the other end of the line, she concluded with a sigh. She forced a cheerful note into her voice. "Hi, Daddy."

She heard a sharp gasp, then absolute silence for a full ten seconds.

"Ashley, is that you?" he asked sharply.

"Yep."

More silence descended. That was followed by a flurry of questions. "What the dickens are you doing answering Dillon's phone and what took so long? Where the devil is he? Are you two at the cabin?"

"We are," she confessed, seeing little point in trying to hide the truth. "Actually, he's in the kitchen cooking lunch. He's very handy to have around."

"If he's so blasted handy," he said sarcastically, "then why didn't he answer his own damn phone?"

"He didn't want to."

Her father chuckled at that. "I see. Typical."

"Did you call for some special reason?"

"I called to see if he was relaxing the way he was supposed to. With you around, though, I doubt that's possible. How'd you end up at the cabin, anyway? I thought you were in New York, fighting off muggers."

"They started fighting back," she said in what had become an old ritual between them. Somehow, though, she couldn't manage her usual teasing note.

"Baby, are you okay?" he asked, his tone sobering as his fatherly antenna kicked in.

"Right as rain," she lied.

"What has that man done to you?" he demanded. "I'll skin him alive if he's hurt you."

"This has nothing to do with Dillon. He just turned up here and found me already hiding out. He's been great. By the way, how did you two become friends?"

"He hasn't told you?"

"Daddy, if I didn't already know his name, I doubt he would have told me that," she grumbled. "He's the most infuriating, tight-lipped man I've ever met."

Her father roared. "So that's the way it is," he said with glee. "By golly, I should have thought of this a long time ago. You and Dillon are perfect for each other. Can't imagine why I didn't see it sooner."

How lovely that he approved, she thought irritably. "Dillon and I are not perfect for each other. We haven't even been here a week and we're already..."

She let her voice trail off as she weighed their quarrels against their lovemaking and decided her father definitely did not need to guess about the latter. She finally settled for adding, "Let's just say we'd drive each other nuts inside of a month."

"Is that your opinion or his?"

"A mutual one, I'm sure."

Her father chuckled. "Maybe I'd better get on home so I can watch this up close."

"Don't tell me you're already bored with all the women in Arizona."

"Didn't say that. But you and Dillon, whoo-ee, that ought to be downright entertaining. Have you burned the cabin down yet with the fireworks?"

"I don't think I should be discussing any fireworks with you," she retorted.

"Probably not," he agreed, though with unmistakable disappointment. "Put Dillon on."

Ashley started down the hall, then hesitated. "What do you intend to say to him?"

"Nothing more than howdy," he swore.

Ashley didn't believe him for a minute. Her father was constitutionally incapable of not meddling. "Maybe I'd better say goodbye, instead. It's been nice talking to you, Daddy. Have fun in Arizona."

"Ashley Wilde, don't you dare hang up on your father," he ordered. "Ashley!"

"Bye-bye," she said cheerfully, cutting him off.

With the cell phone still in hand, she went to the kitchen. She found Dillon at the table, methodically working his way through an omelet the size of his plate and a daunting stack of toast. He glanced up at her return, his expression unreadable.

"Your father, I assume."

Ashley nodded.

"I'll bet he was surprised to find you here."

"Delighted is the word."

His expression turned wary. "Uh-oh."

"Uh-oh is right. He seems to have gotten the crazy notion that you and I, well, that we..."

"Are a match made in heaven," Dillon contributed.

Ashley nodded, then studied him intently. "Which must mean that he really likes you."

"I told you we were friends. Didn't you believe me?"

"More or less."

He shook his head. "Do you always sleep with men you don't entirely trust?"

Something in his sober expression alerted her that the question was far more serious than his deliberately light tone conveyed. How many times did she have to have a red flag waved under her nose before she got the message?

"I never meant to imply that I don't trust you," she said as carefully as if she had one toe in the middle of a minefield and the other foot ready for the next step.

"You didn't imply it. You just about flat-out said it," he said. "You know, ever since we hooked up here, your drawers have been in a knot because you think I haven't been entirely truthful with you, but what about you? There's clearly something going on with you, and you haven't opened up with me. Shouldn't this communication and sharing work both ways?"

Ashley couldn't honestly argue with that. "True," she conceded. "You first."

"Oh, no, you don't. Let's start with a little honesty on your part."

She drew in a deep breath, then nodded. "Okay, what do you want to know?"

"What you're running away from." His tone indicated there wasn't a doubt in his head that she was running from something.

That certainly cut straight to the heart of the matter, Ashley thought. The question was, could she trust Dillon with the truth? Or would it forever ruin his image of her and destroy the desire that stirred in his eyes whenever he looked at her?

She desperately needed the kind of unconditional passion that had existed between them the past few days. Could she risk that for something far more elusive? Despite what her father had said about them being a perfect match, she couldn't see it. Dillon was her rebellion, nothing more. That had to be all there was to it. She surely couldn't have given her heart to a man she hardly knew.

"I'm not running from anything," she said, unable to meet his penetrating gaze when she said it.

"Really?"

There was a world of skepticism in that single word.

"Really," she assured him.

Something that looked an awful lot like disappointment spread across his face. He stood up.

"I think I'll go for a walk."

Ashley's heart began a slow, painful thudding as the distance between them widened. She couldn't let that happen. One of these days the gap would become too wide to bridge, even with spectacular sex.

"Dillon?"

"You're welcome to come along, if you like."

He sounded so cool and removed it scared her. "Are you sure?"

"Why not? A brisk hike will clear our heads, right?"

Ashley was torn. She wasn't sure she could bear the disdain she read in his eyes. But she was terrified to let him out of her sight for fear he'd conclude that whatever had been between them was worth nothing.

When Dillon left the cabin, she fell into step beside him. Once again, he set a brisk, almost punishing pace, though this time he started out downhill. Filled with grim determination, she matched him stride for stride.

"Okay, why don't you just say it?" she asked eventually.

"Say what?"

"Whatever you're thinking. I know you're furious with me."

"Why would you think that?"

"Because you haven't said a word since we left the cabin."

"Because sometimes all words do is lie."

Ashley winced at the direct assault.

He glanced at her. "I'm sorry you feel you can't be honest with me. Now I have some idea what a woman feels like when she's been used."

The comment had the same effect as a slap in the face. She was stunned by the raw hurt in his voice. It was the second time he'd said much the same thing. Ashley recognized belatedly that what she had done in the cabin by shutting him out had been far more devastating to their relationship than the truth might have been.

"Dillon, I had no idea..."

"No idea that the truth could matter to a man like me?" he said bitterly.

"No," she said at once, grasping his hand and jerking him to a halt. "Look at me. It was never that. Never."

"You could have fooled me."

Before she could say anything more, a shot blasted through the air.

"What the hell?" Dillon said. Despite his cold anger, he moved instinctively to protect her, forcing her to the ground. "Could you tell where that came from?"

With her emotions in a tangle, Ashley could barely sort out anything at all, but she nodded. "Over there, I think," she whispered, pointing to a spot to their left.

Another shot split the air, confirming her guess.

"You stay here. I'm going to check it out. There shouldn't be any hunters around in here. The land's posted as private."

"Dillon, don't," she protested. "You're not armed."

He gave her a wry look. "Don't worry about me. I can take care of myself."

Even as the words left his mouth, he slipped into the woods with the skill of a man who knew a lot about subterfuge and silence. Ashley's heart remained in her throat until she heard him call out.

"Ash, it's okay. Over here."

Not entirely certain whether he was being forced to lead her into some sort of trap, she inched her way in the direction of his voice. She found him kneeling on the ground over Mrs. Fawcett, whose ankle was bent at a distinctly odd and clearly painful angle. Ashley rushed to the teacher's other side and knelt down.

"Mrs. Fawcett, what on earth happened?"

"I should think that's obvious," she said testily. "I tripped and fell and broke my darned ankle."

Dillon was gently easing his jacket around her. "How long have you been out here?"

"Overnight," she said, waving off Ashley's shocked response. "I could have crawled to my house, I suppose, but I figured sooner or later someone would come along that trail and I could signal them with my shotgun."

"We need to get you to a hospital," Dillon said in an admirably calm, reassuring tone. "Ashley can stay here with you, while I go to get the car."

"You'll never get the car in here," Ashley pointed out. "And as far as we are from the road, we'd do just as well carrying her to the cabin and going from there."

He nodded. "You have a point. I might not be able to get the car in here, but I can get the Harley."

Mrs. Fawcett's lips thinned, and her chin set defiantly. "I will not be hauled around on that thing like some old sack of potatoes."

"Do you have a better idea?" Dillon asked.

Her gaze assessed him from head to toe. "You look strong enough. You can carry me out of here."

"Like a sack of potatoes?" he asked.

"No, like a lady, young man. I'll have no funny business, either."

Dillon winked outrageously at her. "I may not be able to control myself."

Ashley chuckled at the teasing. It had brightened Mrs. Fawcett's cheeks, so that there was no longer that ashen pallor to her complexion. But when Dillon gently scooped her up in his arms, her face went gray again.

"You okay?" he asked.

"I'll be just fine if you'd get a move on," she said in a voice tight with pain.

Ashley regarded her worriedly. "Mrs. Fawcett, are you sure about this? Maybe Dillon should get the motorcycle."

"I can't imagine why you two are so set on getting me on that contraption, but you can forget about it," she said fiercely.

"I just don't want you passing out on me," Dillon said.

"I won't," she assured him. "I have to keep an eye on you, don't I?"

The two kept up their banter all the way to the house. Ashley's heart swelled with pride at Dillon's cool competence. She was even more impressed with his gentleness and his compassion. It was a whole new side to him that she'd never seen before and never suspected.

When they reached the cabin, Dillon settled Mrs. Fawcett in the back seat of Ashley's car.

"Bring out a quilt and wrap it around her," he instructed. "I'll get her some water. She must be thirsty by now."

"Stop talking about me as if I weren't here," Mrs. Fawcett instructed, her tone as crisp and unrelenting as it had been when asking for algebra homework to be turned in. "Water would be nice, though."

Ashley thought of Dillon's cell phone. "Is there someone you'd like us to call for you, someone who could meet us at the hospital?"

"No, no, I'll be just fine. They'll set my ankle and send me on my way."

Ashley wasn't so sure about that, but she kept her thoughts to herself. She didn't want to butt head-on with the older woman's fierce independent streak. She recognized all too well that it would be a waste of time.

The hospital in Riverton was small, but well-equipped to handle simple emergencies such as this one, thanks to Trent Wilde's generosity.

As soon as the ER staff spotted Ashley and heard the problem, they rushed to the car to assist Dillon with Mrs. Fawcett. Since most of the nurses, as well as the doctor on call, were former students, they treated her with even more deference than usual, Ashley was sure. Nurse Tammy Gates lost focus only briefly when she realized that the man with Mrs. Fawcett was Dillon Ford. Her mouth gaped, but she quickly forced her attention to the patient.

Once Mrs. Fawcett had been taken away for an X ray of her ankle, Ashley looked at Dillon, who seemed suddenly intent on fading into the background.

"Are you okay?"

"I hate hospitals."

He said it with such vehemence that she was startled until she recalled how much time he must have spent in one when his mother was dying with cancer. He'd been an impressionable boy back then, too. Naturally this wouldn't be one of his favorite places.

"Do you want to leave?"

"Not until we see if Mrs. Fawcett's okay. If they do release her, she'll need a way home."

"You were wonderful with her. You were gentle and you kept her distracted."

He seemed so uncomfortable with the praise that she couldn't help asking, "Why does it bother you so when I say something nice about you? Don't you think you deserve it?"

He scowled at that. "Don't play amateur shrink

with me. Maybe I just don't like the surprise I hear in your voice."

Stunned, she simply stared at him. "Surprise? What on earth do you mean by that?"

"It's as if you can't believe I could do anything nice."

"Dillon, that's crazy," she protested, then fell silent as Tammy came out of the back and headed their way. Her attention was focused entirely on Dillon, just as it had been all through high school.

"I can't believe it's you," she said, standing on tiptoe to kiss him squarely on the mouth. "You are a sight for sore eyes."

"You, too, Tammy. It's been a long time."

"Too long," she said adamantly. Belatedly she seemed to remember Ashley's presence. "Ashley, it's great to see you, too. Of course, I feel as if I see you all the time, what with your picture on magazine covers and TV all the time. Congratulations! We always knew you'd be somebody. You had everything it took—beauty, brains and ambition."

Now that Tammy was started, she couldn't seem to stop gushing about Ashley's celebrity status. When she called over one of the other nurses and an aide and introduced her, Ashley was so uncomfortable she wanted to run screaming from the ER. Only years of making public appearances gave her the aplomb to be gracious.

"How is Mrs. Fawcett?" she asked, trying to force the attention away from herself.

"She's doing just fine," Tammy assured them. "Her ankle's a mess, though, and we want to keep her a day or two to be sure there are no aftereffects from her staying out overnight. She's kicking up a terrible fuss over that. Maybe you could talk to her."

"I'll go," Dillon said at once and vanished into the treatment area before Ashley could budge.

Tammy's gaze promptly grew conspiratorial. "So what's between you and Dillon? I was stunned when I saw the two of you walk in here together. You slumming or what?"

Stunned by the unexpectedly crude suggestion, Ashley merely stared.

"Not that he's not the sexiest thing on two feet," she added hurriedly. "I ought to know. I dated him for a whole semester senior year. He was to die for."

"I'm sure your husband will be thrilled to hear you hold such fond memories of another man," Ashley said.

Tammy wasn't the least bit put off by the comment. "Oh, heavens, Whit knows all about Dillon and me. He was Dillon's best friend back then. He figures the end result is all that counts, and he wound up with me."

By default, Ashley guessed, but kept the nasty assumption to herself.

Listening to Tammy, though, had given her some idea of why Dillon got so upset with her reactions to him. Slumming, indeed!

In some ways, she was no better than Tammy. She'd been labeling him since the moment he'd arrived at the cabin, and the label she'd pinned on him had everything to do with the past. No wonder he'd been seething with resentment this morning and on several occasions prior to that.

But hadn't he been doing much the same thing with her? Just like Tammy, he'd been caught up in the myth of Ashley Wilde, superstar model, or alternatively, superstar student. How did anyone ever get past such deeply entrenched images to the real people they hid?

She thought of the way Dillon made her feel and knew with everything in her that somehow she had to try.

Chapter Eleven

Dillon was hiding out, and he knew it. He lingered beside Mrs. Fawcett's bed, forcing a conversation she was too drowsy to participate in beyond an occasional sleepy comment. Anything was better, though, than going into the ER lobby to face Ashley and Tammy.

Seeing Tammy again had brought his past sharply into focus. That possessive spark in her eyes reminded him of the few months when she'd been his girl and his reputation had been at its lowest ebb.

Obviously, she'd managed to turn her life around by going into a respected profession right here in town. He'd fled, certain that memories were too long to forget his outrageous exploits. Maybe he should stick around and ask her how she did it.

Ironically, though Tammy had been very much a

part of his life then, he hadn't felt the same surge of longing to recapture his devil-may-care days he'd experienced when he'd seen Ashley for the first time at the cabin. Tammy stirred regrets, while Ashley brought out hope and possibilities.

"Why are you still here?" Mrs. Fawcett demanded in a groggy voice. "There's no need for you to hover, Dillon. I'm in good hands."

"I know that. Maybe I just like hanging out with you."

"Hogwash," she said succinctly. "Just don't forget to pick me up first thing in the morning. I am not staying in this place one second longer than necessary. It's a waste of good money and hospital resources taking care of someone who can fend perfectly well for themselves."

"Yes, ma'am," Dillon said, grinning at her ability to give orders even when heavily sedated. "I'll be here at ten."

"Make it eight."

"The doctor won't have signed your discharge papers by then," he pointed out.

"Then we'll just leave without them," she said as if they were of no importance whatsoever. "Now, go away. I'm tired and I won't have you watching me while I sleep."

"I'm out of here," he said, then impulsively leaned down and kissed her cheek. "You behave. You're not the boss around here, even if you do remember most of the staff members when they were in diapers."

She smiled at him, her expression a little dreamy

from the knockout dose of sedative she was still fighting. "You're a sweet boy, Dillon. I don't care what anyone says."

"You must be all doped up," he said. "That's a far cry from your usual opinion of me."

"Somebody has to make sure you try to be the best you can, but I've never given up on you. You have a good heart."

He put a silencing finger to her lips. "Don't let that get around, okay?"

"I was always the only one who could see through you, wasn't I?"

Dillon grinned at the smug gleam in her eyes. "I can't imagine how I slipped up with you."

"Does Ashley know what a good man you are?"

"Maybe we should keep that just between you and me," he suggested.

She sighed and closed her eyes, then winked them open again. "Women always fall for the trouble-makers," she told him, "but it never lasts. Tell her, Dillon, before that pride of hers kicks in and it's too late."

Dillon contemplated the advice as he went to the lobby in search of Ashley. He ran into her on her way to join him.

"How's she doing?" she asked.

"Sleeping, finally. I'm to pick her up in the morning at eight, she says. I got the feeling there would be hell to pay if I'm so much as a second late."

Ashley chuckled. "And what does the doctor say?"

Dillon shrugged. "I'm sure he'll do as he's told,

too." He found something in her expression worrisome. "What went on between you and Tammy while I was in with Mrs. Fawcett?"

"Just some reminiscing," she said a little too cheerfully.

He thought of all Tammy could—and would—be likely to say and barely contained a groan. "It was a long time ago," he felt obliged to point out.

Her expression softened. "I know."

"And?"

"And what?"

"You look as if there's more you'd like to say."

"Maybe there is, but I'll save it until we've gone to Stella's for some homemade pie."

Dillon's eyes widened. The small diner was the hotbed of town gossip. For a woman who claimed to crave seclusion, it was not the place to be seen, especially with him. "You want to stop by Stella's Diner? How come? The gossips will have a field day."

"Maybe I'm just hungry."

"Or trying to make a point," he guessed.

"What kind of point would I need to make?"

"That you're not embarrassed to be seen with me."

She looked thunderstruck. "Dillon, I would never be embarrassed to be seen with you. Besides, the only people who matter to me are my family. They already know we're at the cabin together."

That surprised him almost as much as her apparent lack of concern about it. "Someone besides your father knows?"

"By now, yes," she said with a rueful expression. "If Daddy knows, you can bet Dani and Sara know by now, too. Dani was at the cabin the other day, anyway. She knew I was there with a man. She just didn't know it was you or what the circumstances were."

"Because you were embarrassed," he repeated, unable to let old hurts drop so easily.

"Dammit, if you don't knock that chip off your shoulder, I'll just have to do it for you. I didn't tell Dani I was with you because I wanted to keep what was happening between us to myself for a while longer." She leveled those topaz eyes of hers squarely on him. "I don't know how it is for you, but for me it's special. I didn't want to spoil it by having to answer a lot of questions from interested bystanders."

Dillon felt some of the tension drain out of him. His shoulders relaxed. "I see."

"I certainly hope so," she said, "because I really do hate having to explain myself every time I open my mouth."

Dillon grinned. "Then I suppose I'll just have to think of something else to do to keep that mouth of yours occupied," he said, leaning down and crushing it beneath his own.

Oblivious to the possibility of being discovered, oblivious to the antiseptic smells and low beeps of monitors, he kissed her deeply and thoroughly. She tasted of stale vending machine coffee and chocolate. To his way of thinking it was as intoxicating as champagne.

"Been sampling the vending machine offerings, haven't you?" he teased when the kiss finally ended with a sigh of regret from both of them.

"Not that it's any of your business, but yes. I had a craving for chocolate."

"And now you want pie?"

Her gaze narrowed. "Is that a problem for you?"

"Not for me," he assured her. "I think you could do to gain a few pounds. You looked awful scrawny when I got here," he said. He surveyed her thoroughly from head to toe and gave a nod of satisfaction. "I'd say you're coming along nicely now. You look almost healthy again. If we add in a double portion of Stella's peach pie, you'll be just right."

"If only some other people shared your concept of beauty."

She said it in a bitter, defeated way that instantly alerted him that he'd hit a nerve. He wondered if he dared probe for more or if he'd only be rebuffed for his efforts to get at the problem that was nagging at her. He decided to let it go for the moment. Once she had a tummy full of Stella's pie, maybe she'd finally be mellow enough to open up.

Ashley did not like the way Dillon was looking at her. Oh, she loved the approving gleam in his eyes well enough, but not that inquisitive, I'm-getting-to-the-bottom-of-this glint.

Her weight, her food choices, they were all off-limits. As if being tossed out of modeling hadn't been real enough, talking would only belabor it. Even their teasing banter had made her thoroughly self-conscious, so that by the time they walked into the diner, she was certain everyone was staring.

And, of course, they were. Every eye in the place zipped from her to Dillon and back again. People with whom she had once been well acquainted seemed torn between shock and the exuberant welcome that would have been more in keeping with her return home.

When they seemed unable to decide how to react, she settled the matter by waving blithely at everyone in general, then slipping into a booth by the front window. Dillon slid in across from her.

"Not quite the welcome home you envisioned, is it?" he asked sourly. "I'm sorry. It's my fault."

"No," she said vehemently. "It's theirs. Forget them. We came here for pie, not reunions."

"I did," he agreed, studying her intently. "I'm not so sure about you. Are you sure you didn't want to be served your fair share of adulation along with your pie?"

"Dillon," she warned.

"Okay, okay, pie it is." He glanced toward the counter, where the bleached-blond owner of the place was openly staring at them. "Stella, two peach pies and some coffee, please."

Dillon's order spurred the longtime owner of the old high school hangout into action.

"Sure thing, sugar," she said, filling two mugs with coffee, then adding the two slices of pie to her tray.

When she reached the table, she beamed at Ashley. "Bet you're used to fancier places than this by now."

"Maybe so, but I've never had a better piece of pie," Ashley told her honestly. The truth was, she hadn't had any pie in years. Her mouth was already watering at the prospect of Stella's light-as-a-feather crust and sweetened peaches. If only Stella would back off and leave her to eat in peace.

Unfortunately, now that the ice was broken, Stella clearly had a lot of questions. She set her tray on the table beside them and asked Ashley in a low, confidential tone, "Is it true you dated that guy who runs that big car company?"

"Briefly," Ashley said, used to this kind of curiosity, although more often it had come from reporters hoping for a scoop.

"And what about that TV lawyer, the one whose series is such a hit?" Stella asked, eyes wide with envy. "I heard you were dating him, too."

"Briefly," she said again.

"And that king..."

"Actually, it was a prince," Dillon said, startling both women.

Ashley swallowed hard at the suddenly possessive gleam in his eyes. He didn't seem to be overjoyed at the review of her very public dating exploits. He also seemed to know an awful lot about them.

"Been reading the tabloids?" she asked tartly.

"They were hard to miss," he said without the slightest hint of apology. "Even I shop for groceries."

Stella apparently decided wisely that it was time

to beat a hasty retreat. "You let me know if you need anything else," she said as she grabbed her tray and backed away.

Ashley noticed she headed straight for the kitchen, probably so she could get on the phone and call half the town to alert them to the news that Ashley Wilde was back and that she had bad-boy Dillon Ford in tow. Ashley couldn't seem to work herself into much of a frenzy over it. She was too concerned with what everyone's reaction would be if they knew her modeling days were over, that she'd come home a failure.

With a sudden streak of defiance guiding her hand, she ate every bit of the pie Stella had placed in front of her. As she swallowed the last bite, she glanced up and saw that Dillon was regarding her thoughtfully.

"Why did you look as if you were savoring some sort of personal victory rather than that pie?" he asked.

"Because I haven't dared to eat a slice of pie in more than ten years without losing sleep over it," she blurted before she could stop herself.

"Because of modeling," he guessed. "Was your career worth the sacrifices?"

Ashley sighed. "For the past few months, I've been wondering that very thing."

He reached across the table and clasped her hand. "Ashley, what's wrong? Did something happen in New York? Is that why you're hiding out at your father's cabin?"

She could tell from his expression that glib answers were no longer going to cut it. It was time to bite the bullet and spit out the truth. If he thought less of her once he knew, then so be it.

"Okay, here it is." She met his gaze, then looked away, afraid to see his reaction to her revelations. "The short version is that my agent told me I was getting too fat for the sophisticated ads I'd been doing."

Dillon actually laughed at that. "That's absolute, utter hogwash," he declared, then stared hard at her. "You're serious, aren't you?"

"Very," she said, gratified by his response.

"I hope you told him he was nuts."

"Actually, I fired him."

"And came here to lick your wounds."

That awful sense of failure spilled over her again. "Dillon, modeling was everything I dreamed of. I wore incredible clothes. I traveled all over the world. I met fascinating people. I was good at it."

"The best," he concurred. "But that's not who you are. It was just a job."

Just a job, she thought. He made it sound so simple, when the reality was anything but. Her self-worth was totally tied up in her career, in the image of mind-boggling success and physical perfection.

"I wish that's all it was," she said.

"Maybe you should tell me what you think it was."

"It was me. Ashley Wilde, supermodel. People said it in one breath, as if it was part of my name."

"Did any of those people really know you?"

"Well, no, of course not, but—"

"Then why the hell do they matter to you?"

"It's not just them. It's everyone. Right here in Riverton, I was always expected to succeed, and I did it, too. You saw how Stella reacted just now. It's as if she followed my life and took pride in everything I accomplished."

Dillon looked incredulous. "And you think that because you're no longer a model, people here won't think as much of you, that they won't care about you?"

"Something like that." She shook her head. "No, it's more than that. It has to do with the way I think of myself. The photo on the magazine covers, that was me. If all that's over, who am I now?"

"Forget that crackpot agent of yours. You're still beautiful. You're incredibly smart. You have the sexiest little tush in fifty states. You can drive a man wild with one touch of those gorgeous lips. I'd say those are decent attributes to start with."

"You're prejudiced."

"So what if I am? That doesn't make what I say any less true. Maybe it's time to redefine yourself, to think about a new kind of future. Maybe you should look on this not as a failure, which is ridiculous, by the way, but as an opportunity to do something new and exciting and challenging."

"Such as?"

He shrugged. "Whatever you want to do."

"I never wanted to do anything else."

"What about wife and mother?"

Though he said the words nonchalantly, there was an intense gleam in his eyes as he awaited her reaction. Though she loved him for saying those possibilities were open to her, she couldn't envision that path for herself.

She shook her head. "I don't think I'm the type. Dani's the domestic one. Sara's become a real homebody, too. Not me. Settling down never appealed to me. I couldn't wait to get away from Riverton and be somebody."

Dillon's expression was knowing. "And I was practically chased out." His gaze caught hers. "Maybe it's time we paid a visit home again."

"We are home," she reminded him, gesturing to the once-familiar diner where they'd both hung out as teens, albeit with very different crowds.

"No," Dillon corrected. "We've been hiding out in your father's cabin up until today. Maybe it's time we stuck around town and faced the past. It's just possible that instead of letting it control our lives, we can overcome it and set a new course for ourselves."

She regarded him curiously. "You, too? I thought you were comfortable with who you are."

His wry expression said otherwise. "I thought so, too, until I came back here this time. As you've pointed out on more than one occasion, I still seem to be carrying a rather large chip on my shoulder. All it takes is a look—especially from you—and I'm ready to rumble, all those old feelings of inadequacy rampaging around inside me."

"Maybe what Thomas Wolfe said is true," Ashley said thoughtfully. "Maybe you can't go home again."

A spark of pure defiance lit Dillon's eyes. "I say we prove him wrong."

Despite that worrisome gleam, Ashley felt a sudden rush of anticipation. At last a chance to take some action, positive action to get control over her life. "I'm game, if you are. How do we start?"

Dillon's expression sobered. Ashley could practically see the wheels turning in his brain as he considered exactly what they should do first.

"Okay," he said eventually. "Who was the one person in town you felt you had to prove something to? The person whose expectations for you were so high or so outrageous or so misguided that you always felt no matter what you did, you'd come up short?"

"Grace Winston," she said without hesitation, clearly shocking him. Apparently he'd expected her to mention someone in her family, or perhaps a teacher.

"The minister's wife?" he said incredulously.

"Lacey Winston's mother," she corrected. "She always thought Lacey was better than I was and she made sure everyone in the congregation knew that just because I was Trent Wilde's daughter, I was nothing special compared to Lacey. I think she instilled my competitive spirit into me by the time I turned eight. I soared to some of my greatest achievements in Sunday School. Isn't that pitiful?"

"Amazing," Dillon said. His expression turned serious. "Have you actually heard anything about Lacey lately?"

"Not a word. Sara and Dani know better than to mention her name."

"Perhaps we should pay her a visit," he said.

Ashley was startled by the suggestion. "She's still here in town? I thought she'd be a senator or maybe even president by now."

"She's not," he said tersely. He tossed some bills onto the table and held out his hand. "Let's go."

They drove to the edge of town, an area of small, run-down houses with patchy lawns and sagging porches. Ashley's eyes widened as Dillon pulled to a stop in front of a house that was only marginally tidier than the others. Some spark of hope had motivated the owner to paint the shutters a bright red, which were in startling contrast to the faded white of the rest of the house.

"Lacey lives here?"

"She does now. Her husband has been out of work for the past year. According to your father, he's been drinking ever since he lost his job. Lacey works at the Wave and Curl, trying to bring in enough money to keep food on the table. Her parents—her mother in particular—are so appalled by her circumstances that they all but pretend she doesn't exist."

Unexpected tears welled in Ashley's eyes as Dillon added gently, "In your worst nightmare can you imagine your father ever turning his back on you?"

She shook her head. "Never."

"Do you know the real irony? Lacey is happy. I spoke to her a few months ago. Her husband has some skills I could use in my business. I offered him a job, if they'd move to Los Angeles, but she said they like it here. They want to make a go of it in the town where they both grew up. They have family here, roots, and that's important to her.''

''Something I of all people should understand,'' Ashley said. ''Yet I couldn't wait to turn my back on mine.''

''There was nothing wrong with going off to figure out your own identity,'' Dillon pointed out.

''But I didn't. I'm back here more confused than ever.'' She waved off the subject. ''Tell me more about Lacey.''

''She enjoys styling hair, making people feel glamorous and better about themselves. She's a big fan of yours,'' he added, making Ashley feel about two inches tall. ''Your magazine covers are on her walls, and half the women in town have hairstyles copied from your latest pictures.''

Hot tears spilled down her cheeks as Dillon filled her in on the rest of Lacey's story.

''The only thing that really makes her sad,'' he said, ''is the fact that her mother can't see that she has everything she really needs...the love of her husband and her two children.''

Ashley swallowed hard when she saw two towheaded girls run out of the house, laughing as they jumped on their bikes and rode off up the street.

''I suppose you think my problems are terribly shallow,'' she said eventually. ''Heck, even I think they're nothing compared to this.''

''It's not a matter of being shallow,'' Dillon said. ''It's just a matter of perspective. Lacey knows who she is and what she wants. She knows what really matters to her.''

He reached over and wiped away a tear that was tracking down her cheek, then said softly, ''Maybe in that way, she's richer than both of us.''

Chapter Twelve

Eventually Dillon turned the car toward town. Ashley was silent as they drove, thinking of the lesson she could learn from her old nemesis. She was so lost in her own thoughts, it took a long time for one part of Dillon's story to register.

When it did, when she recalled his job offer to Lacey's husband, another puzzle piece fell into place. But, unfortunately, the picture was nowhere near complete. She had figured out by now, though, that Dillon would fill in the rest in his own good time. She also recognized that when he did, it would probably be mind-boggling and miles from anything she could possibly imagine.

"Okay, we've confronted my past," she said. "What about yours? Who do you need to see?"

"Sheriff Pratt," he said immediately.

Ashley simply stared. "You want to pay a call on the sheriff?"

He chuckled. "You say that as if you're worried there might be outstanding warrants for my arrest."

For once he said it without rancor. Maybe he was finally realizing she wasn't judging him, just filled with curiosity at the unexpected twists she was discovering.

"It just seems like an odd choice, that's all," she told him.

"Are you coming with me or not?"

"You aren't planning to get his attention by robbing the bank, are you?"

Dillon shot her a dark look. She grinned at him. "Just a little joke."

"I'm not laughing."

"I can see that."

"No apology?" he taunted.

"Ask me again after we've seen the sheriff."

When they reached the small brick jailhouse, Dillon circled the block.

"There were plenty of parking spaces right out front," she pointed out. "Or were you just checking for the quickest escape route?"

"Have I mentioned that you have a very tart tongue?" he asked as he circled one last time, then pulled into a slot in front.

"Not recently."

"Well, you do. One of these days it's going to get you in a mess of trouble."

"I hope not while we're in the police station. We are going inside, aren't we?"

"In a minute," he said, regarding the building coldly. "I swore I'd never set foot in this place again," he added, almost to himself.

Ashley watched him closely. "Dillon, we don't have to do this. It was just a game."

"Not to me."

She sat back and waited for him to set the pace. He looked as if he was wrestling with the devil, but eventually he drew in a deep breath and turned to her. Evidently he'd made up his mind about something.

"Okay, sweetheart, let's go to jail."

"I hope you don't mean that literally," she said as she climbed out of the car and went with him up the walk. At the entrance, she tucked her hand in his and squeezed. He grinned at her.

"I wish I'd had you beside me for moral support years ago," he said quietly. "Maybe this place wouldn't have terrified me so."

"Me, too," she said and meant it with all her heart.

Inside, the uniformed receptionist at the front desk gaped at the sight of them. Her eyebrows hiked halfway up to her hairline. The reaction was becoming so familiar by now that Ashley barely noticed it.

"We're here to see Sheriff Pratt, Officer," Dillon said. Even as he uttered the words, sweat broke out on his brow.

"It's sergeant," the woman said with surprising antagonism.

Dillon acknowledged the correction with a nod. "Tell him Dillon Ford is here, *Sergeant.*"

"Are you sure?" she said.

She said it with such a conspicuous display of genuine dislike that Ashley couldn't help wondering what the past history between the two might be. She appeared a little old to have been one of Dillon's spurned wanna-be lovers.

The hard line of Dillon's mouth softened ever so slightly at her stunned reaction. "That I'm Dillon Ford or that I want to see the sheriff?"

"Oh, I recognize you, all right," she said, that note of antagonism back again. "But you're the last person I expected to see here." She glanced at Ashley and promptly became more deferential. "Except maybe for you, Miss Wilde."

She looked worriedly from one to the other. "Is there a problem? Maybe I should tell the sheriff what this is about. Miss Wilde, if this man has done something—"

Ashley cut her off. "Maybe you should just tell him we're here," she said cheerfully. "That will be quite enough, I'm sure."

The sergeant shrugged. "If you say so," she said in a dire way that suggested they were signing their own death warrants.

Rather than using the phone to advise the sheriff of their presence, the woman practically ran down the corridor.

"Obviously you impressed the daylights out of her at some point in the past," Ashley noted when she was gone.

Dillon shrugged. "You could say that."

"Care to explain?"

"Actually we had a little tussle over my failure to stop for a red light a number of years ago. She took exception to my decision to flee before she could ticket me."

Ashley groaned. "Dillon, why on earth did you run?"

He winced. "Well, the truth was I was only fourteen. I didn't exactly have a driver's license."

"And you thought if she couldn't ticket you, you wouldn't be in trouble?"

"My thought processes weren't exactly crystal clear back then," he admitted, his expression chagrined. "I was also just the teensiest bit drunk."

Ashley moaned. "Good God. It's a wonder they ever let you out of jail."

"Actually, the sheriff couldn't wait to kick me out. I sang all night long." He grinned. "Have you ever heard me sing?"

"Not that I can recall."

"Oh, you'd know if you had. I can't exactly carry a tune, but I am very enthusiastic. More than one person has pleaded for mercy after listening to me."

Ashley tried to picture a young Dillon, singing to chase away the demons or, more likely, simply to drive the sheriff completely bonkers. She found the image came quite easily, as did an impression of the uptight sheriff's likely reaction. Sheriff Pratt wasn't known for his sense of humor.

"I'm surprised he didn't just lock you away in a soundproof room."

"Believe me, he wanted to, but by then my father and his lawyer had persuaded him to let me go with a stern warning and the promise of parental discipline."

"And did your father discipline you?"

"He beat the tar out of me, actually," he said with startling amusement. "I'd never felt so loved in all my life."

Ashley wanted to weep for the young man who'd had to get into mischief before his father even noticed him. "Oh, Dillon."

"Hey, I didn't bring you here so you'd feel sorry for me," he said. "We're here so I can put all that kind of stuff behind me once and for all."

"I know that, but I can't help it. I wish you'd had a father like mine."

"I do," he reminded her. "Your father all but adopted me a few years later after my own father threw up his hands in defeat. If it weren't for Trent, I'd probably still be trying to prove something by causing trouble."

"Will you tell me how that happened?" she asked as the spit-and-polish sheriff emerged from his office, his anxious sergeant right on his heels.

The ex-Marine strolled toward them with a hard, judgmental expression on his face for Dillon. It softened somewhat when his glance fell on Ashley.

"Miss Wilde," he said courteously. "How's your father?"

"Maybe you ought to be asking Dillon that," she said deliberately. "He's seen him more recently than I have."

"Is that so?" he said, scowling at Dillon. "Why would that be? You rob him blind?"

"No, actually I stopped by to give him a check," he said. "A return on his investment, so to speak."

Ashley stared at him and tried to hide her amazement. Fortunately, the sheriff had plenty of questions of his own. She hoped at least one of them would get her the answers she craved.

"You're telling me that Trent Wilde gave you money?" he asked. "What sort of con were you running?"

Ashley watched as Dillon visibly fought to control his temper. When she gave his hand a supportive squeeze, he shot her a grateful look.

"He didn't give me anything," he corrected in a reasonably calm tone. "He invested in my company." He plucked a business card out of his pocket and handed it over. "Perhaps you've heard of it."

The tough, no-nonsense sheriff stared at the tiny card as if he'd been confronted with a rattler. "You work for Security-Wise?"

Ashley gaped at the mention of the security company's name. She was very familiar with it. Discovering that Dillon was somehow affiliated with it was a real shocker.

Dillon's expression, however, revealed nothing as he said blandly, "I see you've heard of it."

"They handled security when that big movie was being shot outside of town last year. Those guys knew what they were doing, no doubt about that." He regarded Dillon with skepticism. "And you work for them."

"Look again," Dillon suggested.

The sheriff's gaze returned to the business card.

This time his mouth dropped open, much as the receptionist's had earlier. "Says here you're the president."

Dillon nodded. "That's right. President and owner. I'm delighted you were impressed with the men I had working here. They were some of my best."

"Well, I'll be damned," the sheriff said softly, echoing Ashley's amazement, if not her rapidly escalating temper. "If you'd asked me years ago how you'd turn out, I wouldn't have given two cents for the chances of you being out of prison by now."

"Your high regard was excellent motivation," Dillon said sarcastically. "But actually I owe the turnaround to Trent. He believed in me when I didn't believe in myself. All it took was a shove in the right direction."

"I'm glad for you, boy. I truly am." To his credit, the sheriff sounded genuinely sincere.

"Then you won't mind if I decide to move back here and set up shop," Dillon said. "I've been thinking of relocating my headquarters."

Ashley stared, astonished. Why hadn't he mentioned any of this to her? she wondered. Or was this an impulsive statement designed purely to jerk the sheriff's chain?

"I've never had a problem with legitimate business," Sheriff Pratt assured him. "Just monkey business."

Dillon nodded. "Glad to hear it."

He clasped Ashley's hand a little more tightly in a gesture she guessed was meant entirely for the sheriff's benefit. Given the cool reception he'd received, Ashley couldn't entirely blame him for it, though she had a few things she personally planned to get straight with him the minute they were away from here.

"Let's go, sweetheart," he said.

They were almost at the front door when he turned back, halting Ashley in her tracks.

"No hard feelings," he said quietly to the sheriff.

For the first time the sheriff's tight expression eased. "No hard feelings."

"If you ever get tired of your job, I can always use a man with your understanding of the law," Dillon said. A devilish glint lit his eyes as he added, "There are a lot of women in Hollywood who would just love having a man like you as a bodyguard."

The sheriff blushed all the way to the roots of his close-cropped white hair. "I doubt if my wife would go along with that," he said, chuckling. The genuine amusement transformed his face. "But thanks for offering just the same. I suppose I'll go to my grave fantasizing about it."

Outside, Ashley stopped, planted her hands on her hips and glared at the man beside her. "Dillon Ford, you have one heck of a lot of explaining to do."

Making peace with Sheriff Pratt had taken every bit of nerve he possessed, Dillon concluded. Even so, he wasn't sure that was half of what he'd need to make peace with Ashley. She looked mad enough to spit nails. He supposed she had a right.

No, he corrected, gauging the fury in her eyes. There was no supposing about it.

"You seem upset," he said mildly.

"Oh, that's not the half of it, Mr. President of Security-Wise," she said. "Do you know I actually hired one of your people for a shoot last year after there were some threats from an obsessed fan?"

"I know," he admitted blandly. "He really liked you. Said you were a doll."

"He was old enough to be my grandfather."

"He was fifty," Dillon corrected. "And very, very skilled. Had you been hoping for a young stud?"

"Of course not."

"Then I don't see the problem."

"It wasn't a problem," she muttered. "It's just that if I'd known..."

"That I owned the company," he supplied. "What? Would you have gone to somebody else for protection?"

"No. Everyone I asked, including my sneaky, traitorous father, said Security-Wise was the best. I feel as if you lied to me somehow."

"That's absurd. You and I never even talked."

"Which is precisely my point. When the job came across your desk, you knew about it, right?"

He'd expected her to figure that out eventually, but that didn't make admitting it any easier. "Of course," he said reluctantly.

"Then you should have called."

Pleased that she sounded so miffed, he grinned.

"Oh? Why is that? To pamper you? Did you expect special attention given our past history?"

"Of course not."

"What, then?"

"Didn't you even care that I needed protection?"

"Of course, I did. That's why I sent Milt. He's the best in the business. Nobody gets past Milt."

"And what about you? Does anybody get past you?"

"Not if I can help it."

"Then why would you assign someone else to a case you should have taken yourself? Or are you too important to go into the field anymore? Do you just sit back in your fancy office..." She glowered at him. "You do have a fancy office, I assume."

"Very," he agreed. "Plush carpet and leather. The penthouse suite of a very impressive skyscraper, in fact."

"How lovely. So, do you just sit there staring out at the skyline and let other men do the dangerous stuff?"

"Not usually. I take my share of assignments."

"Just not me," she said, looking surprisingly hurt.

"If you'd listen for half a minute, I'd explain."

"Oh, I'm sure."

"Would you please shut up?"

She scowled, but complied.

"Okay, the truth is, you needed somebody to be on the alert every second. I wasn't so sure I could be objective around you. I probably would have had a very hard time keeping my mind on business," he admitted. "The past few days ought to be proof enough that I was right."

That silenced her for a minute.

"I suppose you have a point," she finally conceded.

"I usually do."

She frowned. "You are a very smug man."

"Irritating, isn't it?"

"Damned irritating."

"Do you swear a lot?" he asked. "It's not ladylike."

She shot him a look of disgust. "Oh, for heaven's sake, this from a man who by all rights should have gotten a drunk-driving record at fourteen."

"I knew I shouldn't have told you that. You'll never let me forget it, will you?"

"Does Mrs. Fawcett know? Is that why she won't get anywhere near that motorcycle of yours?"

"I believe she may have been privy to the reason for my absence from school that day." He winked at her. "She thinks I'm cute anyway."

"What does cute have to do with anything?"

"It seems to matter to some women."

"Well, I'm not one of them. I've spent ten years surrounded by cute, gorgeous, sexy men. I was not impressed."

"Then it must be my charm you're falling for."

"Charm?" she repeated incredulously. "What charm? And who says I'm falling for you?"

"Oh, sweetheart, that part is plain as day. The only real question now is what the dickens we're going to do about it."

Color rose in Ashley's cheeks, but wisely, she didn't argue with him. He figured she feared he'd prove his point with another breath-stealing kiss right there on the jailhouse steps. That would knock the socks right off Ms. Sergeant, who was no doubt peering out the window at them at this very moment.

As if to prove his point, he heard the sheriff bellow, "Taylor, get the hell away from that window and get back to work!"

Despite her expressed irritation with him, Ashley started to chuckle. "We do seem to be attracting a lot of attention today, don't we?"

"Everybody's no doubt trying to figure out what you're doing with the town bad boy after you had the chance to nab yourself a prince." He watched her closely. "What is the answer to that, by the way?"

"The prince was a bore," she said succinctly. "And despite some very irritating flaws, you, Mr. Ford, have never been boring."

"I work at that."

Before Ashley could utter the retort that was obviously on the tip of her tongue, Dani came charging down the sidewalk, shirttail flapping, hair mussed and a beguiling smudge of flour on the tip of her nose. She skidded to a halt before them and addressed her sister with fire in her eyes.

"Ashley Wilde, how dare you come into town and not come by to see me?" She glanced at Dillon as if he was an afterthought, then studied him speculatively. "Hello, Dillon. How have you been?"

"Darlin', if I were any better, I'd be sinful."

Ashley rolled her eyes. "Ignore him. He's feeling smug, for some reason."

Dani grinned. "I'll bet I can guess why. The rumor mill is rife with tales of the two of you. Now, quit lollygagging here on the sidewalk and march right on over to my house. You're staying for dinner. I've already called Sara and Jake. They'll be here in an hour."

Dillon chuckled at Ashley's instantly rebellious expression. "Have you always been this bossy?" he asked Dani.

"Always," Ashley confirmed with an air of resignation. "We might as well give in graciously. She won't rest until we're fed and she's pumped us for every bit of information she can about why we're in town together."

"I do not intend to pump you for information," Dani said indignantly. "That wouldn't be proper. Of course, a few polite questions may come up." She winked at Dillon. "Just giving you fair warning."

"You don't scare me," he said. "I remember when I put glue in your chair in the fifth grade and the teacher had to cut your skirt off so you could get free."

Dani stared at him. "That was you?"

"You never guessed?"

Ashley groaned. "Oh, Dillon, you idiot. If she'd guessed, do you think you would have made it out of fifth grade alive? If I were you, I think I'd be very careful about what I ate at her house tonight. The Wildes were raised not to get mad. We just get even. We're very inventive about it, too."

"You're inventive about a lot of things," he observed in a way that had Ashley blushing and Dani choking back laughter. He could tell from the amusement in Dani's eyes that the only way she intended to get even with him was to push her sister squarely into his arms. Obviously she figured that would be torment enough for any man.

Dillon realized with a sense of amazement that he wholeheartedly welcomed the prospect.

Chapter Thirteen

Once Dani had extracted a firm commitment that they would be at her house in time for dinner, Dillon linked hands once more with Ashley.

"We're going to have to work fast if we're going to turn this town on its ear before dinnertime," he told her.

"I thought we'd already done that."

"Not quite. We've just made peace with a few people. There are a few more places I'd like to visit for old times' sake, places I always wished I'd been with you."

Riverton wasn't exactly known for its hot spots, but over the next hour Dillon and Ashley blazed a trail from one end of town to the other, thoroughly enjoying the shocked reactions. In fact, Dillon hadn't had such a good time in years.

Few people in town knew anything at all about the man he'd become with Trent Wilde's encouragement and help. Fewer still cared. Old images died hard. For the first time in years, though, it hardly mattered at all. He realized that, just as he'd been telling Ashley, the only thing that really mattered was what he thought of himself. He knew the kind of man he was.

When he and Ashley walked into the general store, old Mrs. Gates beamed at Ashley and stared hard at him as if trying to decide whether she needed to pull out a shotgun to protect the cash register.

When Ashley caught the woman's behavior toward Dillon, she reacted with such indignation that it brought a smile to Dillon's lips. Sweet heaven, but she was good for him. Despite the nagging doubts she expressed from time to time, he believed with everything in him that she trusted him instinctively. That gut-deep reaction was more important by far than all the reasoned assumptions someone else might make. Next to his faith in himself, hers was the most important.

And oh, how he wanted her. The fierce longing he had felt as a teenager had matured into a powerful need over the past week. The future that had once seemed so impossible glimmered now as a dream that was very much within reach. If he'd believed in love, he would have believed with all his heart this was it.

He was endlessly fascinated by her moods, by the way light caressed her skin, by the way she could look like a sexy waif one minute and a sophisticated lady the next. Her low self-image was so thoroughly absurd that it never even crossed his mind, except in those moments when he witnessed her uncertainties crowding in to dismay her.

Their day in town was like time out of time. Nothing, he thought, could ever spoil the wonder of coming home again with Ashley Wilde on his arm. The way she gazed into his eyes with such trust and admiration and pure yearning meant more to him than all the business accolades he'd earned. In one intense moment, he realized that all he'd struggled to accomplish had been meant to prove something to this woman as much as to himself.

"Do you have any idea how good you are for me?" he asked when they had finally returned to his car and headed a half-hour late for Dani's.

"If it's even half as good as you are for me, then it must be incredible," she said.

The truth of that was plain. The color was high in her cheeks, and her eyes were bright with pure joy. It was the happiest he'd seen her look since his arrival.

"I'm beginning to think you would have been a perfect match for Clyde if Bonnie hadn't gotten to him first," he teased.

"I abhor violence," she said indignantly, then grinned. "But I do rather like being bad."

"You realize, of course, that the only thing bad you've actually done today is to be seen with me."

She sighed. "You're right. I suppose the effect will wear off quickly enough when they discover you're a perfectly respectable businessman and I'm on a downhill slide to nowhere."

The remark made him see red. He jerked the car to the curb and slammed on the brakes. When he'd put the car in park, he framed her face with his hands and said fiercely, "Don't you ever let me hear you say anything like that again, Ashley Wilde. You will always be somebody to me."

She looked a little stunned by his vehemence. "I wish I could see myself through your eyes," she said wistfully.

"You will," he promised, thinking of all the convincing ways he could demonstrate just how beautiful and special she was. "When we get back to the cabin tonight, I will make sure that you see exactly what I see, okay?"

She shivered beneath his touch. Her gaze locked with his. "I can hardly wait."

Now, in the face of that breathless anticipation, it was Dillon's turn to tremble. "Do you think Dani would mind if we didn't show up for dinner?"

She chuckled at that. "Mind? She'd be up at the cabin before we even got the bedroom door closed. No, sweetie, we might as well get on over there and face the inquisition."

"Inquisition?" Dillon said warily.

"If you think that conversation on the sidewalk satisfied her, you're deluding yourself. Add Sara and Jake into the mix and I'd say we're in for a very long evening. We might even have to stay overnight—" she grinned at him "—in separate rooms."

Dillon muttered a curse under his breath.

"My sentiments exactly," she agreed. "Although, Mr. Ford, if you ever expect to get near my bed again, you are going to have to do some very fast talking to explain away all the secrets you've been keeping from me."

He winced at her dire tone. "Maybe we should think about staying in town anyway," he said, hurriedly improvising an excuse. "It's a long drive, and we do have to get Mrs. Fawcett very early in the morning."

"Chicken."

"Just practical," he assured her. "I know how much you love your beauty sleep."

Given the context and her rampaging self-doubts, it was a dangerous thing to say. Ashley reacted by pummeling him in his midsection so hard that all the air whooshed out of him. He stared at her in amazement.

When he could finally catch his breath to speak, he said, "Nice jab."

"I told you I boxed," she said, looking vaguely sheepish.

"You also said you'd never actually hit a person."

"Maybe I just hadn't come across one so desperately in need of being punched before."

Dillon couldn't argue with that, but he reminded himself never to agitate her again and let his guard down at the same time. If word got out that he'd been bested by an untrained woman, his business would go straight down the tubes. Of course, there was one other way to turn her natural skill and fervor in his favor.

He studied her speculatively and wondered if he could convince her to make a drastic career change, give up modeling since it was making her unhappy anyway and become an associate in his firm.

"What?" she demanded. "You're looking me over as if I'm a side of beef you're considering buying."

"Something like that," he said and caught her fist right before it reached his stomach. "Not again, sweetheart."

"Then stop staring."

"I thought you thrived on people staring."

"Not the way you are. Are you going to tell me what that look was about or not?"

"I think not, at least for the moment. A man should have at least one ace up his sleeve when dealing with the likes of you." He started the car. "Now let's go to dinner before your sister comes gunning for us."

If Ashley had had her way, she would have prolonged the moment of their arrival at Dani's for another hour or two, maybe a month or two. She knew exactly the kind of evening they were in for, and she was no more prepared for it than Dillon was. They simply didn't have the sort of answers that would satisfy either of her sisters.

Maybe Jake and Dillon would bond in some protective, male way and keep the cross-examination to a minimum, she thought wistfully. She doubted it, though. No one had ever been able to silence any of the Wilde women when they had something on their minds. Since she personally had flown home to give Jake a fair amount of grief when he and Sara were dating—or more precisely, pretending they *weren't* dating—she doubted he'd be inclined to bail her out.

Naturally, because she and Dillon were late, the whole troupe was waiting at the door for them. Sara caught hold of Ashley's elbow at once and dragged her straight into the kitchen, her eyes flashing with excitement. Ashley caught one last glimpse of Dillon, who seemed a little stunned by their abrupt and unexpected separation.

"That's him, isn't it?" Sara demanded. "The one from high school?"

"I can't imagine what you're talking about," Ashley insisted.

"Oh, fiddle-faddle," Dani said, joining them. "You know perfectly well what Sara means. Everyone knew you had a thing for Dillon back then. At least you had sense enough not to act on it."

"Implying that I no longer have any sense?" Ashley asked testily.

Dani ignored the display of temper. "All I know is that if you wanted to make a grand entrance when you came home to Riverton, you couldn't have picked a better way to do it. The whole town is in an uproar speculating about how the two of you got together. The glamorous cover model and the renegade. It's the stuff of headlines for the *Riverton Weekly.*"

"Is that supposed to bother me?"

Dani and Sara exchanged a look. It was Sara who spoke.

"It always did before. You were the one who always craved approval." She gestured toward the living room. "Dillon Ford is definitely an attention-getter, but I doubt you'll find anyone around who'll sing his praises, unless it's all those women who swooned for him way back then."

"I don't know about that. Daddy seems particularly fond of him," she said casually.

"What?" The astonished gasps came in a chorus.

"It's true," Ashley assured them. "One, they have some sort of bond from way back that Dillon won't say much about, just that he thinks of Daddy like a father. Two, Daddy invested in his company. Three, Daddy loaned him the cabin, which is how we wound up there together. I assumed it would be empty. Dillon turned up a few days later, assuming the same thing."

"Well, I'll be. I wonder what that's all about," Dani said. A speculative glint lit her eyes. "Are you absolutely certain Daddy didn't know you were going to be at the cabin?"

"I know exactly what you're driving at, but no, he wasn't matchmaking. He thought I was in New York. He called the cabin the other day to talk to Dillon. When I answered the phone, he was definitely dumbstruck. Not even he could have faked that reaction."

"Phone?" Sara said. "What phone? Daddy absolutely forbade the installation of a phone up there."

"Dillon has a cell phone."

"My, my, the bad boy has definitely gone mainstream," Sara commented.

"It's more than that," Ashley said dryly. "He actually owns a big-time security company in Los Angeles. I even used one of his bodyguards last year when that crazy fan was threatening me."

"And you didn't know it was Dillon's company?" Dani asked, her amazement plain.

Ashley shook her head. "I didn't have a clue until today, as a matter of fact. I checked them out pretty thoroughly, but everyone seemed to be tight-lipped about the CEO, said he preferred to remain out of the limelight."

"That's a switch. Dillon was never shy," Sara observed. "So, what's the deal between you two? Are you just having a fling to make up for lost time or what?"

Ashley sighed. "I wish I knew."

"Meaning?" Dani wanted to know.

"That I'm so confused these days, I barely know my own name, much less what I'm doing."

"Has he been taking advantage of that?" Dani demanded indignantly.

She looked prepared to march into the living room and take Dillon on single-handedly if that was the case. Ashley gestured for her to settle down.

"He's been an angel, actually. He's boosted my self-confidence. He actually thinks I'm gorgeous."

Sara's eyebrows rose. "Whoever said you weren't?"

Ashley exchanged a look with Dani. "You didn't tell her, did you?"

"I figured that it was up to you to tell anyone you wanted to know."

"Will somebody just tell me?" Sara pleaded.

"I fired my agent. At the moment, I'm no longer modeling."

Sara looked as stunned as if Ashley had announced that she was considering jumping off the Empire State Building attached to a bungee cord.

"You're kidding, right?"

Ashley shook her head.

"But why? You love modeling. You're at the height of your career. I can't walk past a magazine rack without seeing your face."

"Not lately, you haven't. My agent told me I'd gained too much weight. The last thing he offered me was a shoot for a plus-sizes catalogue."

Dani muttered a very uncharacteristic, unladylike oath. Sara echoed it.

"If you got any skinnier a strong wind would carry you away," Sara protested indignantly. "Is he nuts or what?"

"Merely pragmatic, according to him."

"And that's been going on for the past few months?" Sara asked, her expression thoughtful. "So, that's what had you down when you were here for my bronc-riding contest with Jake and again for the wedding."

Ashley nodded.

Sara hesitated, then asked softly, "Can I ask you something?"

"Could I stop you?"

"If all we're talking about is a couple of pounds here, why didn't you just lose it? Heck, you could have afforded to go to some fancy spa and sweat it off."

"Sara!" Dani protested.

"No, she's right," Ashley said. "I've asked myself the same question a thousand times. Goodness knows, I'm familiar with every diet known to man and I belong to the best health club in New York. I should have been able to take it off in a couple of weeks, tops. The only answer I've come up with is that modeling just doesn't matter as much to me anymore as it once did. I seem to be subconsciously rebelling against it."

"Maybe you just got tired of being thought of as a face or a body," Sara suggested. "Maybe you needed to see somebody like Dillon to remember who Ashley Wilde really is."

Ashley thought of the comfort she had felt just being with Dillon and knew at once that her sister was exactly right. It was more than just his appreciative glances, more than his loving touches. It was the fact that he had known her before she became famous, that he had cared for her even then. Dillon had been a godsend in more ways than one. He'd reminded her that there was more to life than rigid self-discipline and deprivation.

"You could be right," she admitted.

"Right about what?" Dillon inquired from the

doorway. He came in and rested a hand on her shoulder. "What are you women plotting in here?"

"Just deciding the future of the world," Sara said blithely.

"Don't believe her," Jake chimed in. "These Wilde women are devious enough left to their own devices. Team the three of them up and a mere man doesn't stand a chance."

"I heard how she landed you," Dillon told the other man. "Didn't sound to me as if you put up too much of a struggle."

"I rode a damned bronco for her," Jake corrected indignantly, "after swearing I'd never get near another one."

"You did that for the ranch, not me," Sara reminded him.

Jake tilted her chin up and planted a noisy kiss on her lips. "It was always a package deal." He glanced pointedly at Dillon. "They have very convenient memories, too."

"So I've noticed," Dillon said, his gaze fixed squarely on Ashley.

She blushed at that penetrating, intimate look. "I think we should go now," she said.

"Now?" All three voices chimed in.

Then Dani added, "You haven't even had dinner yet."

"We haven't?" Ashley asked vaguely, still meeting Dillon's gaze.

"No, and I will be insulted if you don't stay," Dani insisted. Her mouth was set in a determined expression as she added, "Why, I haven't even had a minute to chat with Dillon."

Ashley murmured to the man in question. "You should have helped me out a minute ago. Now you're just going to have to face the music."

He grinned. "Oh, I think I can take anything your sister cares to dish out."

Dani grinned at him and gave a nod of satisfaction. "Good. That's settled, then. If everybody will take a dish into the dining room, I think we can eat."

They'd barely settled down at the table when the doorbell rang. That was followed by an enthusiastic pounding.

"Maybe I'd better get it," Jake said, glancing worriedly in the direction of the front door.

"No," Dani said wryly. "Only one person makes that kind of arrogant commotion."

"Daddy," Ashley and Sara said as they, too, jumped up and headed for the door.

Sure enough, they found their father on the doorstep, scowling at the three of them.

"What's this?" he demanded. "A family reunion and nobody thought to tell me?"

He hugged each of them exuberantly in turn, saving Ashley for last. His sharp gaze searched her face closely before he gave a nod of satisfaction.

"He's being good to you, isn't he?" he whispered in her ear. "If he's not, just say the word, and I'll bust his kneecaps with a crowbar."

Ashley chuckled. "I don't think that will be necessary," she told her father. "I can handle Dillon."

"Oh, can you now?" the very man in question asked from behind her.

By the time Ashley whirled around, he was clasping her father's hand. "It's good to see you, sir. I'm glad you got my message."

Ashley looked from one to the other. Neither looked especially guilty, but that was no doubt because they both had arrogance to spare.

"What message?" she asked.

"I just suggested he might want to come home for a little visit," Dillon said.

Ashley was lost. "Why?"

The two men shared a conspiratorial grin that set her teeth on edge.

"Because he was missing all the fun," Dillon told her.

Ashley was certain there was more to it. So, too, were Dani and Sara, it appeared. They were staring at their father with blatant skepticism.

"What fun?" Dani asked.

"Why, the courtship of these two, of course," their father admitted, hugging Ashley more tightly to one side and clasping Dillon's shoulder with his free hand. "I wasn't about to stay away just when it looked like things at home were going to get downright interesting. As impulsive as these two are, they're liable to run off and get married without me there to give away the bride."

"And what makes you think any courting is going on?" Ashley inquired. She stared at Dillon with a look that could have frozen garden vegetables to be kept for winter meals.

"Actually, it was you who gave me the notion," her father said in a rush.

"Yeah, right," Ashley commented, not believing the sly answer for a minute.

"It was," he assured her a little too heartily. "The way you were tap-dancing around on the phone the other day was a dead giveaway. Got my curiosity up. When I heard from Dillon, it didn't take me a minute to make up my mind."

"And precisely what did Dillon have to say?" Ashley asked.

Dillon wisely avoided her gaze, but her father wasn't the least bit daunted by her icy tone.

"Just that he had you securely on the hook and was about to reel you in," Trent revealed with a spark of pure devilment in his eyes.

Dillon groaned. He was joined in that reaction by everyone in the foyer except Ashley. She simply plucked her car keys out of Dillon's pocket and slammed out of the house, ignoring the denials he was shouting at her.

She didn't stop fuming until she had the car in gear and was halfway down Main Street. Only then did she notice that a car was right on her tail.

When they reached the open road at the edge of town, the car drifted into the oncoming lane and pulled up beside her. She wasn't surprised to see Dillon behind the wheel. Envisioning a head-on collision, she rolled down the window.

"Are you crazy?" she shouted. "Get out of that lane."

"Not until you agree to pull off and talk to me."

"When hell freezes over," she said adamantly and stepped on the gas.

Dillon stayed right beside her, leaving her torn between panic and fury. They probably would have gone for miles that way on the thankfully deserted highway if a police siren hadn't intervened. Ashley groaned as she glanced up and caught the flashing light in her rearview mirror.

"Stupid, stupid, stupid," she muttered as she pulled to the side of the road.

Dillon fell into line right behind her. The sheriff parked behind him. He exited his car and strolled up the highway, shaking his head.

"Well, now, that didn't take long, did it?" he bellowed to Dillon. "Tell me, is there something about Riverton that makes you think you're above the law here?"

Ashley couldn't hear Dillon's response, so it was a huge surprise when the sheriff chuckled. He was still laughing when he backed off and headed toward Ashley's car.

"Out of the car, Miss Wilde," he ordered, his expression stern.

She returned his frosty look evenly. "Excuse me? Dillon didn't have to get out of his car."

His scowl deepened. "Are you questioning my authority?"

"No, of course not. What we were doing was stupid and dangerous. Ticket me, fine me, whatever."

"Oh, I think I've come up with a better way to teach you a lesson, young lady."

She didn't like the sound of that. "He started it," she pointed out. "He was the one driving in the wrong lane."

"He says he was provoked. I believe him."

Ashley stared, incredulous. "You believe him? A few hours ago you were prepared to lock him up without any evidence of a crime at all. You were willing to do it just on general principle."

He gave a curt nod. "Things change. Now march yourself back to his car and climb in."

"I will not," she said, and folded her arms across her middle in a defiant stance.

Dillon's hoot of laughter shot her temper up another notch.

"I think I see the man's problem," the sheriff said. "Now are you going to get in the man's car peacefully or am I going to have to take you into custody?"

She could just imagine the ruckus that would raise in town, especially with her father back to stir things up. There wasn't a doubt in her mind about whose side he'd take.

"Oh, for heaven's sake, I'll go," she muttered, then poked a finger into his barrel chest. "But you'd better plan on retiring after this, because I swear I'll run against you and beat your sorry butt."

Sheriff Pratt chuckled at that. "It'd be worth risking my pension to see that. Now, go on and settle your differences with the man."

She didn't like his patronizing tone, but she bit her tongue. Besides, she wanted to save up all her fury for the man who'd gotten them into this mess.

She climbed into what was apparently her father's rental car. Naturally he'd handed over the keys to Dillon without a qualm. Men!

"Talk fast," she said to him as she slammed the door. "Because when we get out of the sheriff's sight, I intend to strangle you."

He grinned. "Admit it, sweetheart. You haven't had this much fun in years."

"Being chased by a madman and nearly arrested by the sheriff is not my idea of fun," she insisted in a deadly tone.

He glanced over, and his expression sobered. "You were never in any real danger," he assured her. "We never even got above thirty."

"Of course, I know that," she said, waving off the explanation. "That's beside the point." She frowned at him. "What if someone had come around a turn at fifty, Dillon? Did you ever think of that? You could have been killed right in front of my eyes." Even now, the possibility sent a shudder through her.

Shock spread across his face. "You were worried about me?"

"Well, of course, you idiot. I love you," she blurted without thinking. "If you'd gone and gotten yourself splattered across the highway, what would I do then?"

He reached over and pulled her into his arms. "Sweetheart, there was never any chance of that. I would have seen the headlights of any oncoming cars. Besides, almost nobody uses this road."

Ashley was still shaking. "It only takes one, just

one.'' She shivered at the thought of what could have happened. She placed a hand on either side of his face and made sure he was looking straight at her. ''So help me, if you ever do anything that stupid again, you won't have to worry about oncoming cars. I will kill you myself.''

''That will sort of spoil the courtship, don't you think? Your father made that up, but I find I kind of like the idea.''

''There is no courtship,'' she reminded him emphatically. ''Not now and, after tonight, not ever.''

''You just said you love me,'' he reminded her.

''A slip of the tongue, nothing more,'' she insisted over the shouts in her head that for once she had been telling the truth.

''I don't think so.''

She sank back against the seat and crossed her arms again. ''Think whatever you like,'' she said, ''but it will be a cold day in hell before I ever say it again.''

Dillon merely grinned. ''I can wait.''

Chapter Fourteen

It was a very short night, although it seemed like an eternity to Dillon. True to her word, Ashley had banished him to the cabin's guest room. After one last haughty glance, she had vanished into the master suite. She didn't seem to believe that a courtship had been Trent's idea, not his.

Moments later, he'd heard water splashing into that provocative bathtub and envisioned her up to her chin in bubbles. He'd gotten so hard just thinking about it that he was almost tempted beyond endurance to break down the damned door to the suite. He figured he wouldn't earn any points for that, though.

Instead, he paced. He paced the guest room. He paced the living room. And when that began to seem too claustrophobic, he went outside and paced around the cabin in the chilly night air, hoping either to wear himself out or at least to cool his overactive libido.

None of it worked, of course. None of it answered the only question that needed answering. Did Ashley love him enough to marry him?

By morning he was edgy and so grumpy that no one with a grain of sense would have come within a hundred yards of him. Naturally Ashley decided to torment him with a breezy kiss on the forehead and some cheerful little ditty that she hummed off-key until it almost drove him completely crazy.

Dillon watched her as he sipped his fourth cup of coffee in sullen silence.

"Are you about ready to leave?" she inquired, studying him over the rim of her cup.

"Leave?"

"We have to pick up Mrs. Fawcett in an hour. Eight sharp, isn't that what you said?"

"Oh, hell," Dillon muttered, wondering if the day could possibly get any worse. He wasn't prepared to be subjected to the teacher's knowing looks. Unfortunately, he had no choice. He had given her his word.

"It completely slipped my mind," he confessed. "I'll catch a quick shower and be ready to go in ten minutes."

"I could go by myself. You look as if you didn't get much sleep," she said cheerfully.

"I got enough," he lied and headed for the shower.

As he dressed, he thought of all the women he'd

dated who'd been sweet or sexy or uncomplicated. Why couldn't he have fallen for any one of them? Instead he'd had to go and get mixed up with a woman whose slightest glance tied him in knots, a woman so filled with sass and vinegar that he doubted he'd ever have a peaceful moment again.

They made the drive into Riverton in complete silence, while Dillon's stomach churned acid at all the unspoken thoughts careening through him. Ashley kept her gaze fixed on the scenery until they reached the point where her car had been abandoned the night before.

"My car is gone," she announced with a mix of incredulity and fury. "I knew I should never have left it there. Dammit, Dillon, this is all your fault."

"Ash—" he began, but she was on a roll.

"I'm going to sue the sheriff." She glowered at Dillon. "I think I'll sue you while I'm at it."

It was another five minutes before she finally wound down. When she paused long enough to haul in a deep breath, Dillon jumped in.

"May I say something now?"

"I suppose."

"Your father picked up your car."

She stared at him. "How the dickens did that happen?"

"The sheriff took the keys. I called your father. Add it up."

"My father knows about what happened last night?" She winced at the thought of what he would make of that debacle and how enthusiastically he was likely to spread it around town. "Oh, geez, if he knows, then so do Sara and Dani, right?"

"Bingo."

"Well, hell," she muttered in disgust, "I might as well take out an ad in the weekly paper and tell the world that Dillon Ford has turned me into a stark raving lunatic."

"An engagement announcement would be better," he suggested impulsively, wondering exactly which one of them was the craziest. The idea of actually marrying her had to be the most outrageous, most daring scheme he'd ever come up with it. His body hummed in anticipation of success. As soon as the words were out of his mouth, he knew they'd been inevitable. He just had to convince her of that.

"You wish," she commented.

Her attitude only stiffened his resolve. "It's going to happen, Ashley. You could save us both a lot of aggravation by accepting that now."

"Why would I want to save you any aggravation at all?"

"Because if you gave in on this one little point—"

"Getting engaged is a little point to you?"

"Compared to the rest of our lives, yes. Anyway, all I was trying to say was that once we're married, you'd have the rest of your life to torment me at your leisure."

She perked up somewhat at that, then sighed. "No, it would never work. I'd probably just lose interest after awhile."

Dillon stared at her. "Lose interest in tormenting me?"

"No," she said flatly. "In you, period."

It was not a remark designed to cater to his ego. "You can't be serious," he said at once.

"It's true," she said, that defeated note in her voice.

"I think maybe you'd better explain."

"Okay, I loved modeling more than anything, right? I hardly even kissed a boy in high school for fear someone would distract me from my goal. Well, now I've accomplished exactly what I set out to, and look at me. I can't even lose a few pounds so I can keep my job." She shrugged, then added sadly, "The same thing would probably happen with you."

Dillon shook his head to clear the cobwebs and tried to follow her logic. Maybe he'd just been awake too long, but she wasn't making any sense at all. Clearly, though, it all added up to her.

"Okay," he began slowly. "Let me see if I have this straight. You loved modeling. You love me. You fell out of love with modeling, therefore you're going to fall out of love with me."

She scowled. "When you put it like that, it does sound ridiculous, but yes, that's exactly what I'm saying. I don't seem to have any staying power."

"Oh, for heaven's sake," Dillon began, then saw that she was dead serious. "Okay, sweetheart, let's back up a minute. How long ago did you discover that you had feelings for me, maybe not love, but feelings?"

She hesitated. "In high school," she admitted eventually. "But it was just a rebellion, I'm sure, and I wasn't even very good at it. The only thing we ever shared was one dance. I never even had the gumption to kiss you."

He wanted to remind her they had more than made up for it in the past few days, but he restrained himself. "Be that as it may," he said, "the feelings were there, correct?"

"I suppose."

"And they're stronger than ever now, correct?"

"Yes," she admitted, eyeing him cautiously. "What's your point?"

"Doesn't that suggest some sort of staying power to you?"

"I'd wanted to be a model since I turned seven," she countered.

Dillon held back a sigh of pure frustration. "So you figure your fascination with modeling petered out after twenty years or so, and we're just not to that limit yet?"

She beamed at him. "Exactly," she said, then sighed. "Pitiful, isn't it?"

Dillon didn't know whether to laugh or cry. She actually believed the hogwash she was spouting at him. The only way to prove that sort of faulty logic wrong was to hang around for another twenty or thirty years and prove it one day at a time. That would require far more patience than he possessed. A more inventive, aggressive scheme was definitely in order. He thought he had just the right plan to make her admit that she was as crazy in love as he was.

"Ashley," he began, putting the finishing touches on the idea as he pulled to a stop in the hospital parking lot. "We are going to get Mrs. Fawcett, take her home and then you and I are going to do something totally outrageous."

"I don't do outrageous things," she pointed out, despite the spark of fascination that was evident in her eyes.

"You do with me. Just last night you were drag racing me down the old post road."

"Not by choice."

"You could have stopped anytime you really wanted to," he said. "You didn't."

He let that sink in for a moment, then added, "Trust me on this, sweetheart."

She looked as if trust was an alien concept. Dillon held his breath as she appeared to weigh his plea from every angle. Finally, to his relief, she nodded.

"You'll have to do me one favor, though," he said. "You get Mrs. Fawcett checked out and ready to go so I can make a few phone calls, okay?"

"Phone calls?" she asked suspiciously.

"Trust me," he reminded her.

Though she still looked skeptical, she nodded again. Dillon couldn't help wondering if he could pull off his plan while she was still in this compliant mood, or if all her well-honed straight-arrow impulses would kick in at precisely the wrong moment.

As the elevator doors opened on Mrs. Fawcett's

floor, Dillon pushed the hold button and caught Ashley's elbow.

"You do love me, right? Now, at this moment?"

Her gaze caught his and held. Hers was filled with obvious astonishment. "Yes," she said in a voice barely above a whisper.

He nodded in satisfaction. That was all he needed to know to put his plan in motion. The love of a woman like Ashley could inspire a man to reach for the most ingenious schemes of his entire life.

Ashley couldn't shake off the odd sense of lethargy and depression that had come over her the night before. Not even Dillon's promise of an outrageous plan sparked much enthusiasm. She just wasn't the daring type, after all, even if she had once risked her entire future on a chess game. She was still feeling a little lost and out of it when she reached Mrs. Fawcett's room. The sound of her father's booming laughter from inside had her halting in her tracks.

"They are a pair, aren't they?" her father said. "She's stubborn as a mule, and he's got a chip on his shoulder the size of the whole danged state. I can't imagine what it'll be like if..."

The description left little doubt in Ashley's mind that she and Dillon were the subject of the conversation. She supposed she could have stood in the hallway and listened to their opinions, but she didn't have the heart for eavesdropping. She pushed open the door and brought the traitorous chitchat to a halt.

Her father stared at her guiltily, then quickly came to greet her. "Well, hello, baby, I didn't expect to see you at this hour," he said, kissing her soundly on the cheek.

"Dillon and I are here to give Mrs. Fawcett a lift home," she said, still regarding the pair of them dubiously. "What are you doing here?"

"Catching up on old times," Mrs. Fawcett said, blushing like a schoolgirl.

Ashley nodded, though she wasn't entirely convinced that this visit had as much to do with old times as it did with current gossip. "That's right," she said, playing along for the moment. "Daddy was one of your first students, wasn't he?"

"She almost flunked me," her father said indignantly, "even after I told her the reason I couldn't concentrate was that she was so gosh-darned pretty."

"Your sweet talk couldn't make up for not doing your assignments," Mrs. Fawcett said, sounding every bit as prim as she probably had when she'd recited the same words back then. "Besides, a seventeen-year-old boy had no business saying such things to his teacher."

"You were barely twenty-one," he pointed out. "Nowadays, that's hardly cause for anyone to blink."

"I was a teacher. It wasn't right."

He grinned at Ashley. "She was so darned prissy and proper it almost drove me crazy."

"And he was a scoundrel," Mrs Fawcett countered. "Still is, I suspect."

Ashley listened to the banter with increasing amazement. Whatever sparks there had been between them decades ago appeared to be fanning to life again. Once again she had to wonder at the attraction between two such seemingly polar opposites.

Of course, until Mrs. Fawcett had spilled the beans on her father's devilish streak, she would never have suspected it of him. He was a salt-of-the-earth, pillar-of-the-community kind of man. Everyone from the governor on down would have testified to that in a court of law. They would have been shocked by Mrs. Fawcett's assessment of his character.

Just as she doubted if any of Dillon's friends in Los Angeles would believe he had terrorized an entire town in his youth.

The thought came to her like a bolt out of the blue. People were actually a compilation of their images.

What if, like her father, Dillon mellowed into a life of respectability?

And what if she, like Mrs. Fawcett, had a hidden daring streak that could remain alive for a lifetime?

Would those two things make a marriage between her and Dillon more likely to succeed than she had imagined up until now? How could she ever tire of a man who made her senses spin and kept her mind engaged with his unexpected actions? Wouldn't they complement each other? She could keep him from getting arrested, and he could prevent her from dying of total, unrelieved boredom.

All those fiercely protective feelings that had crowded in the day before when she'd observed the reaction of the town's citizens to Dillon's return rose up again. It finally occurred to her that, as badly as she needed him in her life to bolster her flagging self-esteem, he needed her just as much. It wasn't a one-way street at all, she thought with a sudden sense of joy.

"Do you two need me here?" she asked.

"For what?" her father asked blankly, which was answer enough.

"Never mind," she said, grinning at him. She winked at Mrs. Fawcett. "Keep him out of trouble, would you? And be wary of letting him in the front door when he gives you a lift home."

"What would be the fun in that?" the retired teacher replied, her cheeks bright.

"Go find Dillon," her father ordered brusquely, guessing where she was headed and indicating his approval. "A man like that shouldn't be kept waiting forever." His gaze fell on Mrs. Fawcett when he said it. He added softly, "Should he, Tilly?"

Tilly, Ashley thought. She wondered when Matilda Fawcett had ever before been called by such a frivolous nickname. Judging from the pink in her cheeks, it had been thirty or forty years before, and by this very same man.

"Oh, I'd say he's been kept dangling quite long enough," Mrs. Fawcett said pointedly, her gaze locked with Ashley's father's.

Ashley was absolutely certain the remark had far more to do with Trent Wilde than it did with Dillon. She could hardly wait to pass on this momentous tidbit of gossip to her sisters. A romance between her father and Mrs. Fawcett would be a vast improvement over any he might have fallen into during his lonely stay in Arizona.

She knew Jake and Sara had been holding out for some spark to ignite between her father and their longtime housekeeper, but judging from the exchange she'd just witnessed that didn't seem to be in the cards. Besides, she had a feeling Annie knew her father's worst flaws far too well to ever want to marry him.

Forget all that for now, though. First things first. She had to find Dillon and tell him that she would marry him after all.

She searched the hospital from one end to the other, but there was no sign of him. Her stomach sank as she considered the very real possibility that he'd gotten thoroughly discouraged and simply abandoned her to her foolish logic. The phone calls he'd mentioned had probably been no more than an excuse to escape, though she couldn't imagine him running off and abandoning Mrs. Fawcett.

The doubts didn't last long. Dillon had asked her to trust him, and she did.

Since she was completely out of cars at the moment—though it seemed likely that her father had parked hers somewhere in the vicinity—she called Dani to come and get her. There was no answer at her sister's.

Nor was there any answer at Jake and Sara's.

Wasn't anybody in the whole darn family around when she needed them? Well, never let it be said that she wasn't resourceful, she decided, taking off on foot for the center of town. Dani was, no doubt, at the general store delivering a supply of home-baked pies and jams. She'd catch up with her there.

By the time she arrived, though, the pies were at the general store, but there was no sign of her sister. Nor did she find her at home, though the back door was unlocked, as always. Ashley walked in and made herself at home.

Another call to the ranch failed to turn up either Sara or Jake. A call to the hospital was too late to catch her father or Mrs. Fawcett.

"Well, damn," she thought, as she poured herself a glass of lemonade and settled down on Dani's front porch to wait. Sooner or later, somebody was bound to turn up. Dani was too much of a homebody to stay away for long.

Exhausted from her restless tossing and turning the night before, she drifted off to sleep, wondering if she would ever get to tell Dillon the conclusions she'd reached.

She was awakened some time later by the sound of a motorcycle approaching. When she stared down the road, she spotted Dillon, dressed in his usual black from head to toe, though this particular attire appeared to be slightly more formal. Black tie, in fact.

Ashley's eyes lit up. "Nice outfit," she commented, when he pulled to a stop on the lawn in front of her.

He held up a white helmet. "Care to join me? Finding exactly the right helmet took longer than I expected. I came back to the hospital to get you, but naturally you weren't where I'd left you. Your father seemed to think you'd gone looking for me."

"You said you wanted unpredictable. I'm just making sure you get it," she assured him.

"Whatever you say. At any rate, I've been chasing around town ever since, trying to find you."

Something about the white helmet, which was in such stark contrast to his black one, struck her as possibly significant. "Was there some reason the helmet had to be that particular color?"

"Sure," he said with a grin. "As many June fashion spreads as you've done, don't you know that the bride always wears white?"

A huge lump formed in Ashley's throat. "Bride?"

"I thought maybe two daring souls like us should do something totally outrageous, rather than the traditional church to-do. What do you think?"

"Have I said yes?" she asked, even as she left the porch and crossed the lawn. She forced herself to walk slowly.

When she was close enough, he reached out, tucked a finger under her chin and tilted her head until he could gaze straight into her eyes. Apparently he liked what he saw there, because he nodded smugly.

"Yep, I see yes flashing in those incredible topaz sparks in your eyes."

"But has the word crossed my lips?"

He winked. "Not yet, but we'll work on that on the drive to the cabin."

"We're getting married at the cabin?"

"It seemed appropriate."

"Today?"

"Why not?"

"Does anyone know about this?" she wondered. She was pretty sure she already knew the answer. It would explain why no one she'd tried to reach had been home.

"Just family, except for Mrs. Fawcett," he said. "I didn't want to be humiliated in front of anyone else in case you turned me down at the last second and bolted."

"Don't we need a license or something?"

"Your father's Trent Wilde. That cuts through all sorts of red tape."

She chuckled. "Well, God bless dear old Daddy."

"Amen." He regarded her intently. "Are you hopping on or not?"

"I'm thinking about it," she said, considering a lifetime of being caught off guard and lured into doing the unexpected. It was exactly what she wanted, and Dillon was precisely the man to give it to her.

"Stop thinking," he ordered. "Just listen to your heart."

Ashley grinned. "In that case, where's my leather jacket?"

He peeled his off and held it out. "This'll have to do for now. I couldn't find one in white."

Shrugging into the warm leather with its scent of Dillon in every fiber, Ashley felt suddenly complete. This was right. There wasn't a doubt in her mind about it. Dillon filled all the empty spaces in her heart that no amount of acclaim had been able to touch.

"I think black and white go very well together, don't you?" she said, pulling her hair up and tucking it inside the white helmet. She rested her head against Dillon's back and wrapped her arms snugly around his waist. "The contrast keeps things interesting."

"I love you, Ashley Wilde," he said as he kicked the motorcycle into gear.

Ashley thought of the kind of wedding the perfect daughter of Trent Wilde ought to be having, complete with bridesmaids and tons of flowers and organ music and a church filled with all her father's powerful friends.

This outrageous, impromptu ceremony was better. In fact, she couldn't think of a more fitting way to seal the fate of two daring soul mates, one of whom had been lost to predictability for far too long.

"Dillon, you're not going to get too respectable on me, are you?"

"Sweetheart, with you around, there's not a chance of that."

Ashley uttered a small, satisfied sigh and held on tight for what promised to be the ride of her life.

Epilogue

For a man who'd had only a few hours to pull together an entire wedding, Dillon had outdone himself. The front porch of the cabin was lavishly decorated with flowers. Her sisters were decked out in black and white, in keeping with Dillon's apparent theme for the occasion. Her father and Mrs. Fawcett were beaming at the two of them as if they were personally responsible for the union.

Ashley sighed with pleasure at how beautifully it had all come together.

"Everything okay?" Dillon asked, studying her worriedly.

"Never better," she assured him. "You're a miracle worker."

"I had a huge incentive."

"Better be careful, Dillon. You may have trouble coming up with an encore."

"Never," he promised. "You inspire me to new heights. Now go get ready."

Ashley stared at him, appalled. "How? I don't have anything to wear for a wedding."

"Yes, you do," Dani assured her. "Sara and I have taken care of everything. Now let's get busy before the groom gets cold feet."

"Not this groom," Dillon said. "But hurry, though. I'm anxious to close this deal."

Inside, Dani and Sara stood back while Ashley caught her first glimpse of the lace and satin wedding dress hanging in the master suite. Her eyes filled with tears.

"It's Mother's dress," she whispered, recognizing it at once. She turned to Dani. "But she saved it for you. You were always meant to wear it at your wedding."

"I don't seem to be in any big rush to use it," Dani said. "I think she would want you to wear it. She'd hate to think it was just sitting in some dark closet on the biggest day of your life."

"Are you sure?"

"Absolutely. Just don't spill any punch on it, in case my guy ever does turn up."

"He will," Ashley promised, enveloping her oldest sister in a hug. "And he's going to be the luckiest man alive."

Dani wiped away tears and smiled. "I think Dillon and Jake might dispute that. Now come on, before we all start bawling and go to this wedding with our makeup splotched."

"You seem to forget, makeup is something I know a whole lot about," Ashley reminded her.

The rest of the wedding passed in a blur. Ashley was conscious only of Dillon standing tall and proud beside her, and looking so incredibly respectable she found it worrisome.

"You're not going to wear this often," she said, fingering the lapel of his tuxedo once most of the guests had discreetly disappeared. "Not that you don't look handsome, mind you, but I think I like you better in leather." She grinned. "Or better yet, in nothing at all."

Dillon pressed a warning finger against her lips. "Sweetheart, your father is still here."

She glanced across to where her father was whispering into Mrs. Fawcett's ear. "I think he's otherwise occupied. In fact, if that gleam in his eyes is any indication, I think he's dreaming up some outrageous scheme of his own."

Dillon stared. "You don't think...your father and Mrs. Fawcett?"

"Looks that way to me," Ashley said, just as her father stood and headed their way.

"Could I have a word with you, Dillon?" he said.

"Planning on giving him fatherly advice?" Ashley inquired. "Or maybe warning him to treat your daughter right or face the consequences?"

To her astonishment, her father actually blushed. "Not exactly," he muttered. "Dillon?"

Ashley caught her husband's arm. "Wait a second. I think maybe I should hear whatever he has to say."

The inimitable Trent Wilde looked as if he'd been caught sneaking a smoke behind the barn door. "Baby, this has nothing to do with you."

"Then there's no reason not to tell me, is there? And don't give me any of that stuff about guy talk, okay?"

"Damn, but you're stubborn. Dillon, are you sure you can handle her?"

"He cannot, as you put it, handle me," Ashley said. "We are partners, equals. Right, Dillon?"

"Of course, dear," he said dutifully, an amused glint in his eyes that warned her she would pay for his cooperation, especially when it meant lining up against a member of his own gender, and the father-in-law he admired to boot.

"Come on, Daddy," she prodded. "What are you up to?"

"Oh, for heaven's sake," he finally muttered. "If you must know, I was going to ask to borrow the Harley."

"Why?" Ashley and Dillon asked in a chorus.

"Of course, it's yours, if you want it," Dillon added. He handed over the keys to prove it.

Without saying another word to satisfy their curiosity, her father walked away.

"You had to give him the keys before he explained, didn't you? Now we'll never know what's going on."

"I think it's obvious," Dillon said, nodding toward Mrs. Fawcett.

Ashley's father had scooped her up and was heading straight for the motorcycle. The expression on the retired teacher's face was one Ashley recognized all too well—the pure anticipation of a woman who'd waited a lifetime to take risks.

"She wouldn't get anywhere near that thing with me," Dillon said indignantly.

"She's not crazy about you," Ashley pointed out, then patted his cheek. "It's okay, darling, I'll ride with you anytime you say."

He turned her until they were standing thigh-to-thigh. "Always?"

"Even when we're ninety," she promised, just as her father started the Harley and roared off down the driveway. He and Mrs. Fawcett waved just before they disappeared from sight. "I guess he had to come home to figure out how to really kick up his heels."

"He's not the only one," Dillon said. He led Ashley to the porch, sank into a rocker and pulled her into his lap. "I've been thinking about us. I know you claim not to be the domestic type—"

"I'm not," she assured him.

"Could you just listen for two seconds?"

She pressed a kiss to his delectable mouth and promised sweetly, "I'll try."

"I was just trying to say that we don't have to have two-point-two kids, a puppy and a vegetable garden. We can design this marriage any way that suits us. We can travel around the world together on my security assignments. I'll train you, if you're interested, so we can work together. Our kids will grow up with experience in every culture on earth. We can come back to Riverton every now and again just to shock the daylights out of everyone who knew us way back when."

For a woman who'd come home searching for answers, it was definitely a plan, one that appealed to her untapped rebellious streak. She gazed into Dillon's dark eyes and realized it was hard to stir up much rebellion when she was so thoroughly, blissfully content. She grinned at him.

"You told the sheriff you were thinking of opening an office right here. Was that just a spur-of-the-moment jibe, or did you mean it?"

"Not if you'd rather be jetting all over the globe. I'm adaptable."

"You want the truth?"

"Always."

"I think I'd like to come home again. I'd like our kids to be part of a big extended family. I want them to know their grandfather, their aunts and uncles and cousins."

"Cousins? Do you know something I don't?"

"There will be cousins," she assured him. "Sara and Jake are already working on it, and Dani will have babies if she has to adopt a whole flock of them. Something tells me, though, that there's someone just around the corner for her."

"You're just in love with love at the moment."

"True enough," she said, "but I believe it. I found love when I least expected it. So will Dani."

He grinned. "Okay, since you seem to have your sisters' lives all planned out, what about ours? What will you do if we stay here?"

"I was thinking about Lacey."

His amazement was plain. "Your old nemesis? Why?"

"Because of what you said about her wanting people to feel good about themselves. After what I've been through lately, I can see just how worthwhile a goal that is. Maybe she and I can put together some sort of school or retreat for people who want to work on their self-image. With my name—"

"And face," Dillon said.

"Whatever. We should be able to market it."

"I think that's a wonderful idea, Mrs. Ford."

"Do you have any other ideas, Mr. Ford?"

"Just one." He leaned down and whispered in her ear.

"That is definitely the traditional way to start a honeymoon," she agreed.

"Too traditional for the likes of us?" he inquired even as his caresses began to bring her body alive.

Ashley sighed happily as her pulse skittered wildly. "There are some traditions worth keeping," she said. "And this is definitely one of them."

Much later, warm and happy in Dillon's strong embrace, Ashley marveled at how their lives had changed...and how they'd stayed the same. Images and expectations might come and go through the years, but their love, it seemed, was destined to remain constant.

* * * * *

Watch for
DANIELLE'S DADDY FACTOR,
coming April 1997 from
Silhouette Special Edition.

Silhouette's newest series

YOURS TRULY

Love when you least expect it.

Where the written word plays a vital role in uniting couples—you're guaranteed a fun and exciting read every time!

Look for Marie Ferrarella's upcoming Yours Truly, *Traci on the Spot*, in March 1997.

Here's a special sneak preview....

1

Morgan Brigham slowly set down his coffee cup on the kitchen table and stared at the comic strip in the center of his paper. It was nestled in among approximately twenty others that were spread out across two pages. But this was the only one he made a point of reading faithfully each morning at breakfast.

This was the only one that mirrored *her* life.

He read each panel twice, as if he couldn't trust his own eyes. But he could. It was there, in black and white.

Morgan folded the paper slowly, thoughtfully, his mind not on his task. So Traci was getting engaged.

The realization gnawed at the lining of his stomach. He hadn't a clue as to why.

He had even less of a clue why he did what he did next.

Abandoning his coffee, now cool, and the newspaper, and ignoring the fact that this was going to make him late for the office, Morgan went to get a sheet of stationery from the den.

He didn't have much time.

* * *

Traci Richardson stared at the last frame she had just drawn. Debating, she glanced at the creature sprawled out on the kitchen floor.

"What do you think, Jeremiah? Too blunt?"

The dog, part bloodhound, part mutt, idly looked up from his rawhide bone at the sound of his name. Jeremiah gave her a look she felt free to interpret as ambivalent.

"Fine help you are. What if Daniel actually reads this and puts two and two together?"

Not that there was all that much chance that the man who had proposed to her, the very prosperous and busy Dr. Daniel Thane, would actually see the comic strip she drew for a living. Not unless the strip was taped to a bicuspid he was examining. Lately Daniel had gotten so busy he'd stopped reading anything but the morning headlines of the *Times.*

Still, you never knew. "I don't want to hurt his feelings," Traci continued, using Jeremiah as a sounding board. "It's just that Traci is overwhelmed by Donald's proposal and, see, she thinks the ring is going to swallow her up." To prove her point, Traci held up the drawing for the dog to view.

This time, he didn't even bother to lift his head.

Traci stared moodily at the small velvet box on the kitchen counter. It had sat there since Daniel had asked her to marry him last Sunday. Even if Daniel never read her comic strip, he was going to suspect something eventually. The very fact that she hadn't grabbed the ring from his hand and slid it onto her finger should have told him that she had doubts about their union.

Traci sighed. Daniel was a catch by any definition. So what was her problem? She kept waiting to be struck by that sunny ray of happiness. Daniel said he wanted to take care of her, to fulfill her every wish. And he was even willing to let her think about it before she gave him her answer.

Guilt nibbled at her. She should be dancing up and down, not wavering like a weather vane in a gale.

Pronouncing the strip completed, she scribbled her signature in the corner of the last frame and then sighed. Another week's work put to bed. She glanced at the pile of mail on the counter. She'd been bringing it in steadily from the mailbox since Monday, but the stack had gotten no farther than her kitchen. Sorting letters seemed the least heinous of all the annoying chores that faced her.

Traci paused as she noted a long envelope. Morgan Brigham. Why would Morgan be writing to her?

Curious, she tore open the envelope and quickly scanned the short note inside.

Dear Traci,

I'm putting the summerhouse up for sale. Thought you might want to come up and see it one more time before it goes up on the block. Or make a bid for it yourself. If memory serves, you once said you wanted to buy it. Either way, let me know. My number's on the card.

Take care,
Morgan

P.S. Got a kick out of *Traci on the Spot* this week.

Traci folded the letter. He read her strip. She hadn't known that. A feeling of pride silently coaxed a smile to her lips. After a beat, though, the rest of his note seeped into her consciousness. He was selling the house.

The summerhouse. A faded white building with brick trim. Suddenly, memories flooded her mind. Long, lazy afternoons that felt as if they would never end.

Morgan.

She looked at the far wall in the family room. There was a large framed photograph of her and Morgan standing before the summerhouse. Traci and Morgan. Morgan and Traci. Back then, it seemed their lives had been permanently intertwined. A bittersweet feeling of loss passed over her.

Traci quickly pulled the telephone over to her on the counter and tapped out the number on the keypad.

* * * * *

Look for TRACI ON THE SPOT
by Marie Ferrarella, coming to
Silhouette YOURS TRULY
in March 1997.

In the tradition of
Anne Rice comes a
daring, darkly sensual
vampire novel by

As a bonus,
you will also receive
a FREE story by
National Bestselling Author
Stella Cameron,
in the same volume.

MAGGIE SHAYNE

BORN IN TWILIGHT

Rendezvous hails bestselling Maggie Shayne's vampire
romance series, WINGS IN THE NIGHT, as
"powerful...riveting...unique...intensely romantic."

Don't miss it, this March, available
wherever Silhouette books are sold.

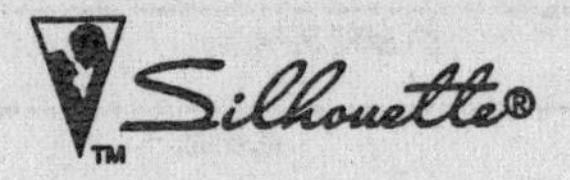

Look us up on-line at:http://www.romance.net

WINGS-ST

Take 4 bestselling love stories FREE

Plus get a FREE surprise gift!

Special Limited-time Offer

Mail to Silhouette Reader Service™

3010 Walden Avenue
P.O. Box 1867
Buffalo, N.Y. 14240-1867

YES! Please send me 4 free Silhouette Special Edition® novels and my free surprise gift. Then send me 6 brand-new novels every month, which I will receive months before they appear in bookstores. Bill me at the low price of $3.34 each plus 25¢ delivery and applicable sales tax, if any.* That's the complete price and a savings of over 10% off the cover prices—quite a bargain! I understand that accepting the books and gift places me under no obligation ever to buy any books. I can always return a shipment and cancel at any time. Even if I never buy another book from Silhouette, the 4 free books and the surprise gift are mine to keep forever.

235 BPA A3UV

Name (PLEASE PRINT)

Address Apt. No.

City State Zip

This offer is limited to one order per household and not valid to present Silhouette Special Edition® subscribers. *Terms and prices are subject to change without notice. Sales tax applicable in N.Y.

USPED-696 ©1990 Harlequin Enterprises Limited

As seen on TV!

Free Gift Offer

With a Free Gift proof-of-purchase from any Silhouette® book, you can receive a beautiful cubic zirconia pendant.

This gorgeous marquise-shaped stone is a genuine cubic zirconia—accented by an 18" gold tone necklace.
(Approximate retail value $19.95)

Send for yours today...

compliments of Silhouette®

To receive your free gift, a cubic zirconia pendant, send us one original proof-of-purchase, photocopies not accepted, from the back of any Silhouette Romance™, Silhouette Desire®, Silhouette Special Edition®, Silhouette Intimate Moments® or Silhouette Yours Truly™ title available in February, March and April at your favorite retail outlet, together with the Free Gift Certificate, plus a check or money order for $1.65 U.S./$2.15 CAN. (do not send cash) to cover postage and handling, payable to Silhouette Free Gift Offer. We will send you the specified gift. Allow 6 to 8 weeks for delivery. Offer good until April 30, 1997 or while quantities last. Offer valid in the U.S. and Canada only.

Free Gift Certificate

Name: ______________________________

Address: ______________________________

City: ______________ State/Province: ______________ Zip/Postal Code: ______

Mail this certificate, one proof-of-purchase and a check or money order for postage and handling to: SILHOUETTE FREE GIFT OFFER 1997. In the U.S.: 3010 Walden Avenue, P.O. Box 9077, Buffalo NY 14269-9077. In Canada: P.O. Box 613, Fort Erie, Ontario L2Z 5X3.

FREE GIFT OFFER **084-KFD**

ONE PROOF-OF-PURCHASE

To collect your fabulous FREE GIFT, a cubic zirconia pendant, you must include this original proof-of-purchase for each gift with the properly completed Free Gift Certificate.

084-KFD

IN CELEBRATION OF MOTHER'S DAY, JOIN SILHOUETTE THIS MAY AS WE BRING YOU

a funny thing
HAPPENED ON THE WAY TO THE
DELIVERY ROOM

THESE THREE STORIES, CELEBRATING THE LIGHTER SIDE OF MOTHERHOOD, ARE WRITTEN BY YOUR FAVORITE AUTHORS:

KASEY MICHAELS
KATHLEEN EAGLE
EMILIE RICHARDS

When three couples make the trip to the delivery room, they get more than their own bundles of joy...they get the promise of love!

Available this May,
wherever Silhouette books are sold.

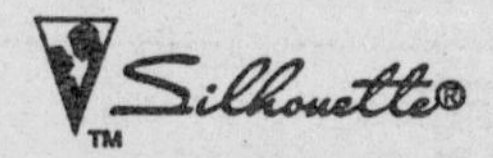

Look us up on-line at: http://www.romance.net

MD

This summer, the legend continues in Jacobsville

A LONG, TALL TEXAN SUMMER

Three **BRAND-NEW** short stories

This summer, Silhouette brings readers a special collection for Diana Palmer's LONG, TALL TEXANS fans. Diana has rounded up three **BRAND-NEW** stories of love Texas-style, all set in Jacobsville, Texas. Featuring the men you've grown to love from this wonderful town, this collection is a must-have for all fans!

They grow 'em tall in the saddle in Texas—and they've got love and marriage on their minds!

Don't miss this collection of original Long, Tall Texans stories...available in June at your favorite retail outlet.

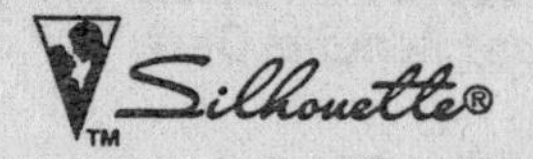

Look us up on-line at: http://www.romance.net

LTTST

You're About to Become a Privileged Woman

Reap the rewards of fabulous free gifts and benefits with proofs-of-purchase from Silhouette and Harlequin books

Pages & Privileges™

It's our way of thanking you for buying our books at your favorite retail stores.

**Harlequin and Silhouette—
the most privileged readers in the world!**

For more information about Harlequin and Silhouette's PAGES & PRIVILEGES program call the Pages & Privileges Benefits Desk: 1-503-794-2499

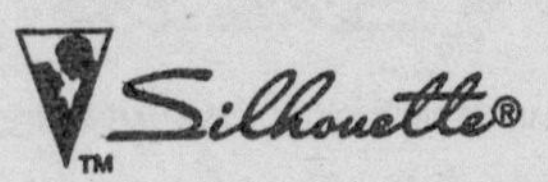

SSE-PP23